THE WEREWOLF

IN GREECE, ITALY, SPAIN AND PORTUGAL

WITH AN ESSAY ON
The Origin of the Werewolf Superstition
BY CAROLINE TAYLOR STEWART

By

MONTAGUE SUMMERS

British Library Cataloguing-in-Publication Data
A catalogue record for this book is available
from the British Library

CONTENTS

MONTAGUE SUMMERS

Augustus Montague Summers was born in Bristol, England in 1880. He was raised as an evangelical Anglican in a wealthy family, and studied at Clifton College before reading theology at Trinity College, Oxford with the intention of becoming a Church of England priest. In 1905, he graduated with fourth-class honours, and went on to continue his religious training at the Lichfield Theological College. Summers entered his apprenticeship as a curate in the diocese of Bitton near Bristol, but rumours of an interest in Satanism and accusations of sexual misconduct with young boys led to him being cut off; a scandal which dogged him his whole life. Summers joined the growing ranks of English men of letters interested in medievalism and the occult. In 1909, he converted to Catholicism and shortly thereafter he began passing himself off as a Catholic priest, the legitimacy of which was disputed. Around this time, Summers adopted a curious attire which included a sweeping black cape and a silver-topped cane.

Summers eventually managed to make a living as a full-time writer. He was interested in the theatre of the seventeenth century, particularly that of the English Restoration, and was one of the founder members of The Phoenix, a society that performed neglected works of that era. In 1916, he was elected a fellow of the Royal Society of Literature. Summers also produced some important studies of Gothic fiction. However, his interest in the occult never waned, and in 1928, around the time he was acquainted with Aleister Crowley, he published the first English translation of Heinrich Kramer and James Sprenger's *Malleus Maleficarum* ('*The Hammer of Witches*'), a 15th century Latin text on the hunting of witches. Summers then turned to vampires, producing *The Vampire: His Kith and Kin* (1928) and

The Vampire in Europe (1929), and then to werewolves with *The Werewolf* (1933). Summers' work on the occult is known for his unusual, archaic writing style, his intimate style of narration, and his purported belief in the reality of the subjects he treats.

In his day, Summers was a renowned eccentric; *The Times* called him "*in every way a 'character'*" and "*a throwback to the Middle Ages.*" He died at his home in Richmond, Surrey.

THE ORIGIN OF THE
WEREWOLF SUPERSTITION

AN ESSAY BY CAROLINE TAYLOR STEWART

The belief that a human being is capable of assuming an animal's form, most frequently that of a wolf, is an almost worldwide superstition. Such a transformed person is the Germanic werewolf, or man-wolf; that is, a wolf which is really a human being. So the werewolf was a man in wolf's form or wolf's dress, seen mostly at night, and believed generally to be harmful to man.

The origin of this werewolf superstition has not been satisfactorily explained. Adolf Erman explains the allusion of Herodotus to the transformation of the Neurians (the people of the present Volhynia, in West Russia) into wolves as due merely to their appearance in winter, dressed in their furs. This explanation, however, would not fit similar superstitions in warm climes. Others ascribe the origin of lycanthropy to primitive Totemism, in which the totem is an animal revered by the members of a tribe and supposed to be hostile to their enemies. Still another explanation is that of a leader of departed souls as the original werewolf.

The explanation of the origin of the belief in werewolves must be one which will apply the world over, as the werewolf superstition is found pretty much all over the earth, especially to-day however in Northwest Germany and Slavic lands; namely, in the lands where the wolf is most common. According to Mogk the superstition prevails to-day especially in the north and east of Germany.

The werewolf superstition is an old one, a primitive one. The point in common everywhere is the transformation of a living human being into an animal, into a wolf in regions where the wolf was common into a lion, hyena or leopard in Africa, where these animals are common; into a tiger or serpent in India; in other localities into other animals characteristic of the region. Among Lapps and Finns occur transformations into the bear, wolf, reindeer, fish or birds; amongst many North Asiatic peoples, as also some American Indians, into the bear; amongst the latter also into the fox, wolf, turkey or owl; in South America, besides into a tiger or jaguar, also into a fish, or serpent. Most universal though it seems was the transformation into wolves or dogs.

As the superstition is so widespread—Germany, Eastern Europe, Africa, Asia, America, it either arose at a very early time, when all these peoples were in communication with each other or else, in accord with another view of modern science, it arose independently in various continents in process of the natural psychical development of the human race under similar conditions.

The origin of the superstition must have been an old custom of primitive man's of putting on a wolf's or other animal's skin or dress, or a robe. Thus Leubuscher, says: "Es ist der Mythenkreis eines jeden Volkes aus einfachen wahren Begebenheiten hervorgewachsen." Likely also the notion of attributing speech to animals originated from such disguising or dressing of men as animals. In the following we shall examine into primitive man's reasons for putting on such a skin or robe.

Primitive man was face to face with animal foes, and had to conquer them or be destroyed. The werewolf superstition in Europe arose probably while the Greeks, Romans, Kelts and Germanic peoples were still in contact with each other, if not in the original Indo-Germanic home, for they all have the superstition (unless, as above, we prefer to regard the belief as arising in various localities in process of psychical development under similar conditions; namely, when people still lived principally by the chase.) Probably the primitive Indo-European man before and at the time of the origin of the werewolf superstition, was almost helpless in the presence of inexorable nature. This was before he used metal for weapons. The great business of life was to secure food. Food was furnished from three sources, roots, berries, animals, and the most important of these was animals. Without efficient weapons, it was difficult to kill an animal of any size, in fact the assailant was likely himself to be killed. Yet primitive man had to learn to master the brute foe. Soon he no longer crouched in sheltered places and avoided the enemy, but began to watch and study it, to learn its habits, to learn what certain animals would do under certain circumstances, to learn what would frighten them away or what would lure them on. So at least the large animals were to early man a constant cause of fear and source of danger; yet it was necessary to have their flesh for food and their skins for clothing.

Very soon various ingenious contrivances were devised for trapping them. No doubt one primitive method was the use of decoys to lure animals into a trap. Some could be lured by baits, others more easily by their kind. Occasionally masks were used, and similarly, another form of the original decoy was no doubt simply the stuffed skin of a member of the species, whether animal or bird, say for example a wild duck. Of course the hunter would soon hit on the plan of himself putting on the animal skin, in the case of larger animals; that is, an individual dressed for example in a wolf's skin could approach near enough to a solitary wolf to attack it with his club, stone or other weapon, without exciting the wolf's suspicion of the nearness of a dangerous foe. So the animal disguise, entire or partial, was used by early man acting in the capacity of a decoy, firstly, to secure food and clothing. Secondly, he would assume animal disguise, whole or partial, in dancing and singing; and both these accomplishments seem to have arisen from the imitation of the motions and cries of animals, at first to lure them, when acting as a decoy. With growth of culture came growth of supernaturalism, and an additional reason for acquiring dance and song was to secure charms against bodily ills, and finally enlivenment. In both dance and song, when used for a serious purpose, the performers imagined themselves to be the animals they were imitating, and in the dance they wore the skins of the animals represented.

Probably as long as animal form, partial or entire, was assumed merely for decoys and sport (early dancing), for peaceful purposes therefore, such people having whole or partial animal shape were not regarded as harmful to man, just as wise women began to pass for witches only when with their art they did evil. A similar development can be traced in the case of masks. It was some time before man could cope with food- and clothing-furnishing animals that were dangerous to life, though these are the ones he first studied; and we cannot presuppose that he disguised to represent them until he could cope with them, since the original purpose of the disguise was to secure food and clothing. Thus far then we see whole or partial disguise as animals used to secure *food* and *clothing* when acting as decoys to lure animals; and in *dancing*.

Fourthly, primitive man would put on an animal's skin or dress when out as *forager* (or robber) or *spy*, for the purpose of avoiding detection by the enemy. The Pawnee Indians for example, were called by neighboring tribes *wolves*, probably not out of contempt, since it may be doubted that an Indian feels contempt for a wolf any more than he does for a fox, a rabbit, or an elk, but because of their adroitness as scouts, warriors and stealers of horses; or, as the Pawnees think, because of their great endurance, their skill in imitating wolves so as to escape detection by the enemy by day or night; or, according to some neighboring tribes, because they prowl like wolves, "have the endurance of wolves, can travel all day and dance all night, can make long journeys, living on the carcasses they find on their way, or on no food at all." ... And further, "The Pawnees, when they went on the warpath, were always prepared to simulate wolves.... Wolves on the prairie were too common to excite remark, and at night they would approach close to the Indian camps." ... The Pawnee starting off on the warpath usually carried a robe made of wolf skins, or in later times a white blanket or a white sheet; and, at *night*, wrapping himself in this, and getting down on his hands and knees, he walked or trotted here and there like a wolf, having thus transformed himself into a common object of the landscape. This disguise was employed by *day* as well, for reconnoissance.... While the party remained hidden in some ravine or hollow, one Indian would put his robe over him and gallop to the top of the hill on all fours, and would sit there on his haunches looking all over the country, and anyone at a distance who saw him, would take him for a wolf. It was acknowledged on all hands that the Pawnees could imitate wolves best. "An Indian going into an enemy's country is often called a wolf, and the sign for a scout is made up of the signs *wolf* and *look*." Should any scout detect danger, as at *night* when on duty near an encampment, he must give the cry of the coyote.

The idea of the harmfulness to other men of a man in animal form or dress became deeply seated now, when men in animal disguise began to act not only as decoys for animals dangerous to life, but also as scouts (robbers—and later as possessors of supernatural power, when growth of culture brought with it growth of supernaturalism); when people began to associate, for example, the wolf's form with a lurking enemy.

All uncivilized tribes of the world are continually on the defensive, like our American Indian; they all no doubt on occasion have sent out scouts who, like our American Indians, to avoid detection, assumed the disguise of the animal most common to the special locality in question, just as to-day they are known to disguise in animal skins for purposes of plunder or revenge.

The kind of animal makes no difference, the underlying principle is the same; namely, the transformation of a living human being into an animal. The origin of the belief in such a transformation, as stated abovewas the simple putting on

11

of an animal skin by early man. The object of putting on animal skins was,

(1) To gain food. For this purpose the motions and cries of animals were imitated (origin of dancing and singing), artificial decoys (like decoy ducks to-day) and finally even masks were used.

(2) To secure clothing in cold climes by trapping or decoying animals, as in (1) above.

(3) The imitation when decoying, of the motions of animals led to dancing, and in the dances and various ceremonies the faces and bodies of the participants were painted in imitation of the colors of birds and animals, the motions of animals imitated and animal disguises used.

(4) Scouts disguised themselves as animals when out foraging, as well as for warfare, therefore for booty, and self-defense. Either they wore the entire skin, or probably later just a part of it as a fetich, like the left hind foot of a rabbit, worn as a charm by many of our colored people to-day.

(5) For purposes of revenge,, personal or other. For some other personal motive of advantage or gain, to inspire terror in the opposing agent by hideousness.

(6) To inspire terror in the opposing agent by symbolizing superhuman agencies. So now would arise first a belief in superhuman power or attributes, and then,

(7) Witchcraft. It is very easy to see why it was usually the so-called medicine-men (more correctly Shamans), who claimed such transformation power, because they received remuneration from their patients.

(8) Finally dreams and exaggerated reports gave rise to fabulous stories.

We have discussed (1), (2), and (3); for an example under (4) we have cited the practices of American Indians. It is probable that about now (at the stage indicated in (4) above), what is known as the real werewolf superstition (that of a frenzied, rabid manwolf) began to fully develop. The man in wolf-skin was already a lurking thief or enemy, or a destroyer of human life. To advance from this stage to the werewolf frenzy, our primitive man must have seen about him some exhibition of such a frenzy, and some reason for connecting this frenzy particularly with, say the wolf. He did see insane persons, and the connecting link would be the crazy or mad wolf (or dog, as the transformation was usually into a wolf or dog,) for persons bitten by it usually went mad too. The ensuing frenzy, with the consternation it occasioned, soon appealed to certain primitive minds as a good means of terrorizing others. Of these mad ones some no doubt actually had the malady; others honestly believed they had it and got into a frenzy accordingly; others purposely worked themselves up into a frenzy in order to impose on the uninitiated. Later, in the Middle Ages, when the nature of the real disease came to be better understood, the werewolf superstition had become too firmly fixed to be easily uprooted.

We have discussed (5), (6), (7), and (8) in the notes. As further examples of the development into fabulous story, we may cite any of those stories in which the wild werewolf, or animal-man is represented as roaming the land, howling, robbing, and tearing to pieces men and beasts, until he resumes his human form. Thus an early scout in animal garb would be obliged to live on food he found on his way, and later fabulous report would represent him as himself when in disguise possessing the attributes of the animal he represented, and tearing to pieces man and beast. For such an account see Andree, concerning what eyewitnesses reported of the wild reveling over corpses of the hyena-men of Africa. Naturally the uninitiated savage who witnessed such a sight would become insane, or at least would spread abroad such a report as would enhance the influence of the hyena-men far and wide. Some savages, as in Africa, came to regard any animal that robbed them of children, goats or other animals, as a witch in animal form; just as the American Indians ascribe to evil spirits death, sickness and other misfortunes.

We can see how at first the man in animal disguise or an animal robe would go quietly to work, like the Pawnee scout; how though, as soon as the element of magic enters in, he would try to keep up the illusion. At this stage, when the original defensive measure had become tainted with superstition, men would go about in the night time howling and holding their vile revels. Andree, narrates how a soldier in Northeast Africa shot at a hyena, followed the traces of blood and came to the straw hut of a man who was widely famed as a magician. No hyena was to be seen, only the man himself with a fresh wound. Soon he died, however the soldier did not survive him long. Doubtless one of the magician class was responsible for the death of the soldier, just as we to-day put to death the man who so violates our laws, as to become a menace to our society, or as formerly kings killed those who stood in their way; or as religious sects murder those who dissent from their faith. These magicians, supposed to be men who could assume animal form, as a matter of fact do often form a class, are greatly feared by other natives, often dwell with their disciples in caves and at *night* come forth to plunder and kill. It is to their interest to counterfeit well, for if suspected of being malevolent, they were put to death or outlawed, like criminals to-day. Their frenzies were, as said above, in some cases genuine delusions; in other cases they offered, as one may readily imagine, excellent opportunities for personal gain or vengeance.

Only by instilling in their fellows a firm belief in this superstition and maintaining the sham, could the perpetrators of the outrages hope to escape punishment for their depredations, could they hope to plunder and steal with impunity. So they prowled usually under the cloak of *night* or of the dark of the forest, howled and acted like the animals they represented, hid the animal skin or blanket, if they used one, in the daytime where they thought no one could find it, whereas the animal skin which was worn for defence, was put on either by day or night, and one story recounts the swallowing of a whole goat, the man bellowing fearfully like a tiger while he did it. Some of the transformed men claimed they could regain human form only by means of a certain medicine or by rubbing. The imposters were the criminal class of society that is still with us to-day, no longer in werewolf form, but after all wolves in human dress, each maintaining his trade by deception and countless artifices, just as did the werewolf of old. Not unlike these shams are those of the American negro, who in church, when "shouting," that is, when stirred up by religious fervor, inflicts blows on his enemy who happens to be in the church, of course with impunity; for he is supposed to be under some outside control, and when the spell has passed off, like some of the delusionists mentioned, claims not to know what he (or generally she) has done. Similar also are the negro voudoo ceremonies, those of the fire-eaters, or any other sham.

The wolf disguise, or transformation into a werewolf was that most often assumed for example in Germanic lands. The term *wolf* became synonymous with *robber*, and later (when the robber became an outlaw,) with *outlaw*, the robber and outlaw alike being called wolf and not some other animal (i. e., only the wolf-man surviving to any extent) firstly, because the wolf was plentiful; and secondly, because as civilization advanced, there came a time when the wolf was practically the only one of the larger undomesticated animals that survived. We can notice this in our own United States, for example in eastern Kansas, where at night coyotes and even wolves are sometimes heard howling out on the prairie near woodlands, or in the pastures adjoining farms, where they not infrequently kill smaller animals, and dig up buried ones.In Prussia also it is the wolf that survives to-day. American Indians, and other savages however do not restrict the transformations to the wolf, because other wild animals, are, or were till recently, abundant amongst them. As civilization advances, one by one the animal myths disappear with the animals that gave rise to them (like that connected with the mastodon); or else stories of such domestic animals as the pig, white bull, dog superseded them. When this stage was reached, as time went on and means of successfully coping with the brute creation became perfected, the animals were shorn of many of their terrors, and finally such stories as Aesop's fables would arise. This however was psychologically a long step in advance of our were-wolf believing peoples of an earlier period.

Up to this point the illustrations have shown that the werewolf superstition went through various stages of development. The motives for assuming wolf's dress (or animal skins or robes), at first were purely peaceful, for protection against cold, and to secure food by acting as decoys; then it was used for personal advantage or gain by foragers (or robbers) and spies; then for purposes of vengeance; later from a desire for power over others; and finally men (the professional and the superstitious) began to concoct fabulous stories which were handed down as tradition or myth, according to the psychic level of the narrator and hearer.

The starting point of the whole superstition of the harmful werewolf is the disguising as some common animal by members of savage races when abroad as foragers or scouts, in order to escape detection by the enemy. Like wolves they roamed the land in search of food. As stated above, later fabulous report would represent them as possessing in their disguise the attributes of the animal they impersonated, and finally even of actually taking on animal form, either wholly or in part, for longer or shorter periods of time. Some of the North American Indian transformation stories represent men as having only the head, hands and feet of a wolf. The transformation into a werewolf in Germanic lands is caused merely by a shirt or girdle made of wolf-skin. This shirt or girdle of wolf-skin of the Germanic werewolf is the survival of the robe or mantle originally disguising the entire body. It would be but a step further to represent a person as rendering himself invisible by putting on any other article of apparel, such as the Tarnkappe. The stories especially in Europe were of the *were-wolf* rather than *were-bear* or other animal, because the wolf was the commonest of the larger wild animals. It was the stories of the commonest animal, the wolf, which crystallized into the household werewolf or transformation tales.

GREECE, ITALY,
SPAIN AND PORTUGAL

$\mathbf{F}$AR to the north of Europe, as the ancients knew it, in the centre of the region which now comprises Poland and Lithuania, about the river-basin of the Bug, dwelt the nomad Neuri, a mysterious and wellnigh unknown folk who were reputed enchanters of mickle might (γόητες), as, indeed, are the Shamans among Siberian vagroms of to-day. Concerning the Neuri, the Father of History, Herodotus of Halicarnassus (484–c. 404), writes in his Fourth Book, *Melpomene* [1] : " The Neuri have the same customs as the Scythians. In the generation before that land was invaded by Darius the whole nation was forced to migrate on account of the plague of serpents, since not only did their own territory produce very many, but even vaster numbers thrust in on them from the deserts of the north. Being thus tormented they abandoned their native soil and took refuge with the Budini. It appears that the Neuri are sorcerers, and such they are confidently held to be both by the Scythians and by the Greek settlers in Scythia, who relate that once every year each Neurian becomes a wolf for a few days, and then again resumes his original form. This, however, they will never persuade me to believe, although they assert it roundly and confirm their statement by a solemn oath."

Pomponius Mela, in his *De Situ Orbis, Of the Situation of the World*, II, i, follows Herodotus : " The Neures haue a certaine time to euerie of them limitted, wherein they may (if they wil) be chaunged into Woolues, and returne to their former shape againe." [2]

Herman Hirt, *Die Indogermanen*, I, i, 18, " Das Baltisch-Slavische," remarks : " Wir können die Neuren nicht einmal mit Sicherheit für einen slavischen Volksstamm halten. Man sieht in ihnen eigentlich nur deshalb Slaven, weil von den Neuren berichtet wird, dass sich jeder einmal in einen Wolf verwandle, worin offenbar die Sage vom Werwolf verleigt. Abu wenn diese Sage auch bei den Slaven weit

19

verbreitet ist, so ist sie doch nicht auf diesen Volksstamm beschränkt. Ausserdem hat man den Namen *Neuren* mit dem slavischen Worte *nurija* 'territorium' zusammer gebracht, aber dies ist sicher aus dem Griechischen ἐνορία entlehnt." [3]

The attempted explanation of Adolf Erman,[4] who ascribes the metamorphosis of the Neuri into wolves as a legend due to their appearance in the winter months wrapped in thick furs, is trivial to the last degree. It is very plain that werewolfism was rampant among this boreal tribe of witches.

Pausanias, in the Eighth Book of his *Description of Greece*, a section which must have been written after A.D. 166, and was indeed probably composed at least a decade later,[5] when dealing with Arcadia, speaks of the werewolfism still prevailing in those districts. So important is his testimony to these magical rites that the pertinent passages must be quoted in full : " The Arcadians say that Pelasgus was the first man who lived in this land . . . Pelasgus' son Lycaon outdid his father in the ingenuity of the schemes he projected. For he built a city Lycosura on Mount Lycaeus, he gave to Zeus the surname of Lycaean, and he founded the Lucaean games. . . . In my opinion Lycaon was contemporary with Cecrops, king of Athens. . . . Cecrops was the first who gave to Zeus the surname of Supreme,[6] and he refused to sacrifice anything that had life. . . . Whereas Lycaon brought a human babe to the altar of Lycaean Zeus, and sacrificed it, and poured out the blood on the altar ; and they say that immediately after the sacrifice he was turned into a wolf. For my own part I believe the tale : it has been handed down among the Arcadians from antiquity, and probability is in its favour. . . . They say that from the time of Lycaon downwards a man has always been turned into a wolf at the sacrifice of Lycaean Zeus, but that the transformation is not for life ; for if, while he is a wolf, he abstains from human flesh, in the ninth year afterwards he changes back into a man, but if he has tasted human flesh he remains a beast for ever." [7]

In chapter xxxviii of the same book Pausanias describes Lycosura, which he deems the oldest of all cities on earth. To the left is Mount Lycaeus, the Sacred Peak of Arcady. Actually Lycosura, which was excavated 1889–1895, is about five miles from Mount Lycaeus, of which I made the ascent from the little village of Karyaes or Isioma. The journey occupies three-quarters of an hour to an hour, the traveller passing through a most attractive country. To-day Mount Lycaeus is known as Diaphorti or Mount S. Elias, from a chapel dedicated to that Saint,[8] which is built near the summit. There are two peaks, the higher being Stephani; whilst the lower, Mount S. Elias, is the ancient Lycaeus. Here is an artificial platform strewn with blocks of stone and other fragments plainly marking the site of the temple of Zeus Lycaeus, which must (I suppose) be one of the most terribly haunted places in the world. The summit is about a quarter of an hour from the simple shrine of the Saint, to whose protection those ascending as far as the top will do well to commend themselves in all sincerity.

The panorama spread out beneath as one gazes from the crest of the mountain is indeed magnificent, a landscape extending over the broad plains of Megapolis, Elis, and Messenia, whilst to the west the sea is visible as far as Zakynthos.

Extremely significant is the reserve of Pausanias as he goes on to speak concerning the worship on that Mount: " Of the wonders of Mount Lycaeus the greatest is this. There is a precinct of Lycaean Zeus on the mountain and people are not allowed to enter it; but if any one disregards the rule and enters, he cannot possibly live more than a year. It is also said that inside the precinct all creatures, whether man or beast, cast no shadows[9]; and, therefore, if his quarry takes refuge in the precinct, the huntsman will not follow it, but waits outside, and looking at the beast he sees that it casts no shadow . . .

" On the topmost peak of the mountain there is an altar of Lycaean Zeus in the shape of a mound of earth, and most of Peloponnese is visible from it. In front of the altar, on the east, stand two pillars, on which there used formerly to be gilded eagles. On this altar they offer secret sacrifices to Lycaean Zeus, but I do not care to pry into the details of the sacrifice. Be it as it is and has been from the beginning."[10]

" Very evil was the beginning," justly comments Sir William Ridgeway,[11] for Lycaon, son of Pelasgos, sacrificed a human babe to the demon there. Not without reason has it been suggested that the Zeus who was secretly worshipped with ritual bloody and obscene upon the mountain heights of Arcady may well have been some Semitic Baal imported by Phœnicians from the Syrian groves and hills.[12]

Arcadia itself was the cradle of the human family, primitive tradition aversed. The people who dwelled there were the oldest of all races, elder brothers of the sun and moon.[13] Their land was enclosed on all sides by great ranges, Cyllene and Erymanthus, Artemisius, Parthenius, and dread Maenalus, the sanctuary of Pan.[14] Fabled Alpheus, that stream which in his course sank beneath the earth, rose at Phylace. The story of Lycaon takes us back to remotest antiquity, to the days before a flood covered the world, the age of the Giants and the Titans, for Lycaon was the son of Pelasgos, who was the son of Mother Earth. And it was when Nyktimos, the son of Lycaon, ruled in his father's room that the deluge of Deucalion overswept the continents.

We have seen what Pausanias has to say of the sacrifice of Lycaon, but other authors give different stories. Apollodorus in his *Bibliotheca*[15] relates that Lycaon, the son of Pelasgos, was by many wives the father of fifty sons,[16] whose names he duly chronicles.[17] Now these sons were impious and proud above all other men. In order to prove them, under the guise of a wayfarer weary and seeking hospitality Father Zeus visited their palaces, and in mockery they slew a child at the hest of cruel Maenalus, commingling his warm entrails with the savoury mess they served up to the guest. But then in wrath the god arose, and overturning the table—whence the place is called Trapezus (Τραπεζοῦς) to this day—he blasted King Lycaon and his son with the red levin bolt. Nuktimos, the youngest, alone was spared, for old Mother Earth stayed the hand of the angry god.

Hyginus, in his *Fabulae*,[18] says that Zeus sought hospitality with Lycaon, the son of Pelasgos, being fired with love for the king's daughter Callisto, whom he presently enjoyed, and Arcas was born. In the *Poeticon Astronomicon*[19] the same author has it that Arcas was sacrificed by Lycaon, as also Eratosthenes tells in the *Catasterismoi*.[20] Lycaon was turned into a wolf, his sons struck by the thunderbolt.

In the *Alexandra*[21] of Lycophron are two lines :

GREECE, ITALY, SPAIN, & PORTUGAL

χερσαῖος αὐτόδαιτος ἐγγόνων δρυὸς
λυκαινομόρφων Νυκτίμου κρεανόμων,

upon which the old scholiast, whose work was so ably used by Isaac and John Tzetzes, glosses allowing two versions of the tale, either that when Lycaon and his sons had mingled the boiled flesh of Nuktimos with the fare set before Zeus the outraged deity turned them all into wolves, or that he destroyed them with thunder and Mother Earth alone prevented him from ravaging all Arcady.[22]

Nicolaus Damascenus,[23] the friend of Augustus Caesar and Herod the Great, knows yet another version of the story. In his *History* he tells that Lycaon himself was righteous, but that his sons were impious and profane. Sleeveless was his warning that Zeus in the form of a stranger every day assisted at the solemn sacrifice. In evil jest they slew a child and mingled his members with the meat offered upon the altar, saying, " Let the god discern ! " Whereupon consuming fire fell upon them from heaven.

Ovid in the *Metamorphoses*, book i,[24] makes Jupiter speak thus to the synod of Olympus :—

> The Clamours of this vile degenerate Age,
> The Cries of Orphans, and th' Oppressor's Rage
> Had reach'd the Stars ; I will descend, said I,
> In hope to prove this loud Complaint a Lye.
> Disguis'd in Humane Shape, I Travell'd round
> The World, and more than what I hear'd, I found.
> O're *Mœnalus* I took my steepy way,
> By Caverns infamous for Beasts of Prey :
> Then cross'd *Cyllenè*, and the piny shade
> More infamous, by Curst *Lycaon* made.
> Dark Night had cover'd Heav'n and Earth, before
> I enter'd his Unhospitable Door.
> Just at my entrance, I display'd the Sign
> That somewhat was approaching of Divine.
> The prostrate People pray ; the Tyrant grins ;
> And, adding Prophanation to his Sins,
> I'll try, said he, and if a God appear
> To prove his Deity, shall cost him dear.
> Twas late ; the Graceless Wretch, my Death prepares,
> When I shou'd soundly Sleep, opprest with Cares :
> This dire Experiment, he chose, to prove
> If I were Mortal, or undoubted *Jove* :
> But first he had resolv'd to taste my Pow'r ;
> Not long before, but in a luckless hour
> Some Legates, sent from the *Molossian* State,
> Were on a peaceful Errant come to Treat :

23

THE WEREWOLF

Of these he Murders one, he boils the Flesh;
And lays the mangl'd Morsels in a Dish:
Some part he Roasts; then serves it up, so drest,
And bids me welcome to this Humane Feast.
Mov'd with disdain, the Table I o're-turn'd;
And with avenging Flames, the Palace burn'd.
The Tyrant in a fright, for shelter, gains
The Neighb'ring Fields, and scours along the plains.
Howling he fled, and fain he wou'd have spoke;
But Humane Voice, his Brutal Tongue forsook.
About his lips, the gather'd foam he churns,
And, breathing slaughters, still with rage he burns, ⎫
But on the bleating Flock, his fury turns. ⎬
His Mantle, now his Hide, with rugged hairs ⎭
Cleaves to his back, a famish'd face he bears.
His arms descend, his shoulders sink away,
To multiply his legs for chace of Prey.
He grows a Wolf, his hoariness remains,
And the same rage in other Members reigns.
His eyes still sparkle in a narr'wer space:
His jaws retain the grin, and violence of face.

According to Ovid, then, the tyrant Lycaon in order to
test the power of his visitor places before him at a banquet
the flesh of a Molossian whom he has foully slain, mingled
with the baked meats of the day. The outraged deity
destroys his palace in flames and transforms him to a howling
wolf. Crime upon crime are heaped upon the head of Lycaon,
who in Ovid's poem outrages every law human and divine.
We do not know how far Ovid modified or altered the incidents
of his story, nor indeed from what author he may have
derived it nor under what form.

We are on surer ground with Pliny, who in his *Naturall
Historie*, book viii, chapter xxii, adds further important
details. The passage in question is as follows : " That men
may be transformed into wolves, and restored againe to their
former shape, we must confidently believe to be a lowd lie,
or else give credit to all those tales which wee have for so
many ages found to be meere fabulous untruths. But how
this opinion grew first, and is come to be so firmly setled,
that when wee would give men the most opprobrious words
of defiance that we can, wee tearme them *Versipelles* (i.e. Turn-
coats), I thinke it not much amisse in a word to shew.
Euanthes (a writer among the Greekes, of good account and
authoritie) reporteth, that hee found among the records of
the Arcadians, That in Arcadia there was a certain house

24

and race of the *Antæi*, out of which one evermore must of necessitie be transformed into a wolfe : and when they of that familie have cast lots who it shall be, they use to accompanie the partie upon whome the lot is falne, to a certaine meere or poole in that countrey : when he is thither come, they turne him naked out of all his clothes, which they hang upon an oke thereby : then he swimmeth over the said lake to the other side, and being entred into the wildernesse, is presently transfigured and turned into a wolfe, and so keepeth companie with his like of that kind for nine yeeres space : during which time, (if he forbeare all the while to eat mans flesh) he returneth againe to the same poole or pond, and being swomme over it, receiveth his former shape againe of a man, save onely that hee shall looke nine yeeres elder than before. *Fabius* addeth one thing more and saith, That he findeth againe the same apparele that was hung up in the oke aforesaid. A wonder it is to see, to what passe these Greekes are come in their credulitie : there is not so shamelesse a lye, but it findeth one or other of them to uphold and maintaine it. And therefore *Agriopas*, who wrote the Olympionicæ, telleth a tale of one *Dæmœtus Parrhasius*, That he upon a time at a certain solemne sacrifice (which the Arcadians celebrated in honour of *Iupiter Lycæus*) tasted of the inwards of a child that was killed for a sacrifice, according to the manner of the Arcadians (which even was to shed mans blood in their divine service) and so was turned into a wolfe : and the same man ten yeeres after became a man againe, was present at the exercise of publicke games, wrestled, did his devoir, and went away with victorie home againe from Olympia. Over and besides, it is commonly thought and verily beleeved, that in the taile of this beast, there is a little string or haire that is effectuall to procure love, and that when he is taken at any time, hee casteth it away from him, for that it is of no force and vertue unlesse it be taken from him whiles he is alive. He goeth to rut in the whole yeere not above twelve daies."

For the sake of the flavour and the vigour of his phrase I quote old Philemon Holland's translation of Pliny,[25] but there are one or two points which call for amendment. In the first place it must be noted that the name *Fabius*[26] is due to following a corruption in the MS., and the passage

25

should more correctly run : " He addeth one thing more."
There are several variants of the name *Agriopas* ; Kalkmann
and Mayhoff both prefer Apollas ; Gelenius has Agriopas ;
Jahn and Detlefsen conjecture Copas or Scopas.

Unfortunately it is impossible to identify the authors
whom Pliny quotes. Evanthes may be the historian of
Miletus who is mentioned by Diogenes Laertius [27] ; or
Evanthes of Samos to whom there is a single reference in
Plutarch [28] ; or yet again Evanthes, the author of μυθικά,
who is spoken of by the Scholiast on Apollonius Rhodius.[29]
He may even be another Evanthes concerning whom nothing
is known. Owing to the corruption of the MSS. as noted
above it were idle to attempt to guess the date of Agriopas
or Apollas or Scopas, whichever name it is selected to read.

M." Terentius Varro Reatinus, " Romanorum doctissimus," [30] in the *Antiquitates Rerum Diuinarum*, which was
the second part of his great work *Antiquitatum Libri*, than
the loss of which there have been few more serious misfortunes
to scholarship, dealt in some detail with shape-shifting and
is quoted by S. Augustine in the *De Ciuitate Dei*, XVIII, xvii,
where the holy Doctor speaks of " Pan Lycaeus " and
" Iuppiter Lycaeus ", both of whom were worshipped in
Arcadia, and whose cults had some mysterious connection
with the metamorphosis of men into wolves, a transformation
" which could only be wrought by some supernatural power ".

S. Isidore also mentions the " sacrifice which the Arcadian
offered to their god Lycaeus, and of which whosoever partook
was changed into beastial shape ".[31]

Solinus, it may be remarked, who echoes Varro in his
account of Arcadia, writes briefly " in qua montes Cyllene
et Lycaeus, Maenalus etiam diis alumnis inclaruerunt ", but
curiously enough he does not refer to the wolf-cult or to any
shape-shifting.[32]

Professor Robertson Smith thought that the worship of
this god on Mount Lycaeus was the cult of a wolf-clan, and
that Zeus Λύκειος was the god of the clan. Thus Lycaon,
who sacrifices his son and is changed into a wolf, " may
darkly figure the god himself." [33] This theory is provisionally
allowed as possible by Dr. Farnell and Sir William Ridgeway,
both of whom, however, justly show a marked reluctance to
press it too far. Dr. Farnell writes [34] : " The strangest, and

in some respects, most savage was the Arcadian worship of Zeus on Mount Lycaeum, a worship that belonged to the pre-historic period, and continued at least till the time of Pausanias without losing its dark and repellent aspect . . . it was chiefly as a god who demanded and received human sacrifice that Zeus Lyceius was known and dreaded . . . The human sacrifice is a noteworthy fact of very rare occurrence in the worship of Zeus . . . The rite of human sacrifice on Mount Lycaeum, and at Alus, whatever its original significance may have been, seems to have become connected with a sense of sin and the necessity for expiation, that is, with the germ of a moral idea. We might perhaps be able to say how far this conception of Zeus Lycaeus, as a god who demanded atonement for sin, advanced to any spiritual expression, if the ode of Alcman that commemorated this worship had been preserved."

Sir William Ridgeway writes of the sacrifices to Zeus Lycaeus [35] : " It is possible that the story of the transformation of some one of those present into a wolf may have arisen from the circumstance that as the medicine-men of modern totem clans often get themselves up like their totem animal, so the priest who officiated at the Lycaean rite may have arrayed himself in a wolf-skin."

H. D. Müller [36] suggested that the belief in Arcadian lycanthropy may have arisen from dramatic representations and dancers dressed in wolf-skin about the altar of the god. This theory is wholly untenable.

Mons. G. Fourgères sums up a very ample study *Lykaia* [37] (τα Λύκαια) by setting forth three explanations which have been advanced concerning the cult of Zeus Lycaeus :—

(1) The worship is that of a sun-god, originally from Egypt or Phœnicia, where the wolf is a symbol of light. Or the deity is a god of the underworld, the name being derived from a root *vl'g*, to rend or tear (cf. *lupus*, *luperci*, and the Etruscan *lupu* which is *dilacerator*).

(2) The cult is that of a god who was worshipped on high places, and is of Semitic origin, imported by a Phœnician race, to which the human sacrifice pretty clearly points. The sanctuary then is of the Syrian Maabeds, and Zeus Lycaeus is the same as Baal-Louki, a Moloch cult such as Baal-Libau, Baal-Hasios, and Baal-Hermon.

THE WEREWOLF

(3) The cult is that of a totem. The wolf-god was the primitive deity of the aborigines of Arcadia, in which case the human sacrifices were the cannibalistic feasts of a tribe of wolf-men whose totem was the wolf.

Although I will not attempt to decide definitely between these three suggested origins, and it is indeed an inquiry unessential to the point in view, it seems more probable that Zeus Lykaios may indeed be regarded as a Baal of the Moloch cult, such a god as was worshipped " upon high mountains, and hills "[38] (super montes excelsos et colles) with bloody and obscene rites, a deity who was in truth a demon of hell.

There is an allusion in Plato's *Republic*, book viii, to the Arcadian cult as follows : " What are the first steps in the transformation of the champion into a tyrant ? Can we doubt that the change dates from the time when the champion has begun to act like the man in that legend which is current in reference to the temple of Lykaean Zeus in Arcadia ?

" What legend ?

" According to it, the worshipper who tasted the one human entrail, which was mixed up with the other entrails of other victims, was inevitably metamorphosed into a wolf. Have you never heard the story ?

" Yes, I have.

" In like manner, should the people's champion find the mobile so very compliant that he need make no scruple of shedding kindred blood, should he . . . render himself blood-guilty, making away with human life, and tasting the blood of his fellows with unholy tongue and lips defiled . . . is it not thenceforth the inevitable destiny of such a man either to be destroyed by his enemies, or to become a tyrant, and so to be transformed from a man into a very wolf ? "

Strabo in his *Geographica*, viii, 888,[39] notes that in his day, the reign of Augustus Cæsar, the sanctuary of Zeus Lykaios was wellnigh deserted.

It should be mentioned, moreover, in connection with the rites of Mount Lycaeus that Zeus was under one aspect regarded as an elemental power, a rain god, for in times of drought the Arcadian wizard ascended to the summit of the mountain and propitiated the god by certain sacrifices and ceremonies thus ensuring the rain.[40] The authors of the

Figvre de la Beste feroce que l'on nomme l'hyéne qui a devoré plus que 80 personnes dans le Gevaudan.

A — F.
à Manson 1765

A Representation of the Wild Beaſt of the Gevaudan, who is ſaid to have devoured upwards of 80 Perſons. From a drawing made in April 1765 in the hands of Mr. ——— Kennedy.

THE WILD BEAST OF THE GEVAUDAN
(See p. 235)

29

GREECE, ITALY, SPAIN, & PORTUGAL

Malleus Maleficarum, part ii, question 1, chapter 15,[41] tell how devils and their disciples can cause rain and storm, disturb the air and raise up winds, and give us many examples of the same. Remy in his *Demonolatry*, book i, chapter xxv,[42] explains that witches have the power of raising the clouds and shaking them down in rain on the earth. Guazzo, also, in his *Compendium Maleficarum*,[43] book 1, chapter vii, shows that " It is most clearly proved by experience that witches can control not only the rain and the hail and the wind, but even the lightning when God permits ". Very many other authorities might be cited to the same effect, for there is a profusion of evidence. The Arcadian priests, then, were deeply versed in black magic.

The cult of Zeus Lykaios, the human sacrifice, the killing of babes,[44] the werewolfism, and in fact every detail may be exactly paralleled in the worship of the Satanists, and there can be no doubt that among the Arcadians sorcery and witchcraft were rife, the synagogue of the witches being Mount Lycaeus.

The wolf is very closely and very mysteriously connected with yet another Panhellenic deity, the god Apollo, to whom it may at the outset be noted that human sacrifice was offered at Leukas and in Cyprus.[45] In the Dorian epoch the Argives worshipped Apollo Lykaios, $Λύκειος$.[46] Dr. Farnell even ventures to say that the wolf is far more intimately at home in the legend and ritual of Apollo $Λύκειος$ than in the legend and ritual of the Arcadian Zeus $Λυκαῖος$.[47] Be that as it may, and whatever the real derivation of the epithet $Λυκαῖος$, it is clear enough that werewolfism even if not an original circumstance of the worship of Arcadian Zeus on Mount Lycaeus, was at any rate soon grafted into that horrid liturgy. When Leto was in her pains the wolves led her, who was in the form of a she-wolf,[48] from the Hyperboreans of the north to the isle of Delos [49]—some say to the river Xanthos [50] in Lycia—and then she gave birth, whence Pandaros in the *Iliad* [51] calls Apollo " Son of the She-Wolf ", $Λυκηγενής$.[52] The wolf shape was on occasion assumed by the god. As a wolf he destroyed the wizard Telchiries [53]; as a wolf he covered Kyrene, who bare him Aristaios.[54] The Wolf was sacrificed to Apollo at Argos,[55] and " being then the familiar animal, and at times the sacrificial victim, it is probable that the wolf was in some way regarded as 'the double' or the incarnation of the deity ".[56]

Ælian states that the people of Delphi worshipped the wolf,[57] Clement of Alexandria mentions that divine honours were paid to the wolf by the Lycopolites, and according to the Scholiast on Apollonius Rhodius,[58] "the wolf was a beast held in honour by the Athenians, and whosoever slays a wolf collects what is needful for its burial."

It seems probable that it was as Λύκειος, the wolf, that the god first pronounced his oracles and assumed his mantic character.[59]

Various later legends were invented to explain the term Wolf-god, such as that which said that when Apollo served Admetus it was his task to kill the wolves who molested his flocks,[60] or that when Athens was infested by wolves he bade the citizens sacrifice on the site of the Lyceum, and there they dedicated a temple to the god since the smell of the holocaust had driven the animals from the spot.[61] At Sikyon, too, there was a shrine of Apollo Lykaios, who had counselled the Sikyonians to mingle the bark of a certain tree with meat and set it out for the marauding wolves. They did so, and the beasts were poisoned by the bark. The tree they laid up in the sanctuary of the Wolfish God, but no man knew of what wood it was.[62]

Dr. Farnell hints that it is not impossible that the Attic hero Λύκος, whose statue as a wolf stood near the law-courts, was merely a degenerate form of the god. In the *Heroicus* [63] of Philostratus Apollo Lykaios is named Φύξιος, but this perhaps can hardly be pressed to mean that the wolf-god protected the exile, although if such were the case we find an interesting parallel in the laws of the Franks and Normans, among the Anglo-Saxons and in later England,[64] and it is certain that the connection between the wolf and outlawry is of very ancient date.

That werewolfism was practised in the worship of Apollo as in the cult of Arcadian Zeus can hardly be doubted. It was an old temple of Apollo, surrounded with a grove in which certain sorcerers and idolators continued their abominable rites on the summit of Monte Cassino, that S. Benedict destroyed in 529 to build two fair chapels there under the invocation of S. Martin and S. John. Round about the ancient pagan oratory " upon all sides there were woods for the service of devils, in which, even to that very time, the mad multitudes of infidels did offer most wicked sacrifice ".[65] Although not expressly stated, it seems more than probable that werewolfism was practised here amid the foul mysteries of the demon.

Driven underground or lurking only in the darkest and dustiest corners, werewolfism yet persisted, and now and again we catch a curious half-glimpse of these abominations. Such a one is afforded accidentally enough in the Byzantine tale which finds a place among the *Fabulae Aesopicae*.[66] This collection was made in the fourteenth century by the Basilian Maximus Planudes, one of the most learned of the Constantinopolitan monks of the last age of the Greek empire under Andronicus II and III Palaeologi. It is impossible even to guess at the date or locality of the original story. A cunning thief put up at a certain wayside hostelry in the hope that he might be able to spring a partridge or two. After some shiftless days he noticed that mine host in a tearing-fine cloak (for it was a festa) had sat him down on a bench by the inn door. The road was empty, and so Prince Prig sits him down too and begins a comfortable gossip. After a bit slyboots yawns horribly and utters a dismal howl. Mine host soon inquires what a pox the matter may be. " I' faith, cummer," answers his companion, " you shall know. First, however, I am going to ask you to keep a sharp eye on my clothes for me. I protest I cannot tell why I should be seized with these sudden gapings and yawns, for my sins I shouldn't wonder, or on some other old account, I can't imagine what. But after I have yawned thrice, just like that, hey presto ! I turn into a huge wolf— one of those beasts that gobble men in a trice, bones and all." At this up jumps mine host in a very great hurry, and is rubbing off fast enough. But the thief clutched tight of his cloak, bawling out, " Pray, good sir, wait a bit until I give you my clothes, for I don't want to miss 'em." As he spoke, he nearly cracked his jaws with gaping a third time. Whereon mine host, little minded to be made a meal of, in a sad fright bolted rous through the door, which he took good care to double lock and bar behind him, leaving his cloak to shift for itself. So the budge nims the togeman, and Prince Prig is off on his way to see more of the world. Moral : We must not believe everything we hear.

From the frank simplicity of this little tale we can judge how constant was the belief in shape-shifting and what a very real and present danger the werewolf was conceived to be.

In the year 1542 Constantinople was so plagued by werewolves that Solyman II, " the Magnificent," at the head of his Janizaries, led an attack against them and destroyed no less than 150 of these monsters who were prowling the streets and lanes of the city. Nor is this at all strange if we consider the terrible doom of Constantinople less than a century before, when amid unspeakable cruelty and carnage an Imperial City of the Christians became the capital of the Ottoman Empire, the monasteries were violated, the churches turned into mosques, and incontinently under the rule of the turban the rank weeds of magic flourished and grew most luxuriantly. Our authority for this incident is Job Fincel, a German physician of the sixteenth century.[67] Born at Weimar, he studied philosophy at Wittemberg, and medicine at Jena, where he proceeded Doctor in 1552. At this University he occupied the Chair of Philosophy, and was afterwards aggregated to the Faculty of Medicine. However, he soon returned to Weimar, where he practised as a consulting physician until 1568, after which he resided at Zwichau in the same capacity. He died at this town, but the date is uncertain. He wrote a *De Peste*, Wittemberg, 8vo, 1598, and his elegant Epithalamium *In Nuptiis Dauidis Chytræi* may be found in the *Delitiae Poetarum Germanorum*.[68] His most important work is the *Wunderzeichen, Warhafftige, Beschreibung und gründlich verzeicnus schrecklicher Wunderzeichen und Geschichten, die von . . . MDXVII. bisauff . . . MDLVI. geschechen und ergangen sind, noch der Jarzal . . ,* Jhena, 1556.

Throughout the centuries lycanthropy has been known to the Greeks, and it is terribly prevalent in Eastern Europe to-day, a horrid legacy from Arcadia of old, so difficult is it to eradicate the foul arts of sorcery, so sleepless is Satan in his craft.

The Rev. H. F. Tozer, in his *Researches in the Highlands of Turkey*,[69] writing upon " The Vrykolaka, or Eastern

Vampire ", remarks : " Mr. Baring Gould in his ' Book of Were-Wolves' has spoken of the *Vrykolaka* as if it was identical with the were-wolf, and says that those who are believed to be lycanthropists during life become vampires after death. This, however, is, I think, a mistake. In the great majority of cases the were-wolf superstition is wholly independent of this belief ; so much so, that one writer, who has carefully collected the authorities on the subject, expresses his opinion that the nature of the were-wolf is no longer to be recognized in the modern Greek *Vrykolaka*.[70] Among the Wallachians, however, there is a kind of *murony* that corresponds to the belief in kynanthropy, which is one of the forms of the same superstition. This is described as ' a real living man, who has the peculiarity of roaming by night as a dog over heaths, pastures, and even villages, killing with his touch horses, cows, sheep, swine, goats, and other animals in his passage, and appropriating to himself their vital forces, by means of which he has the appearance of being in continual health and vigour '.[71] The name of this being, the *priccolitsch*, is evidently another form of *vrykolaka* ; from which it is probable that the modern Greek belief was once connected with the same notion, more especially as the idea of lycanthropy was well established among the Greeks in classical times. Indeed, if we may believe M. Cyprien Robert,[72] this same belief is also found as a form of vampirism in Thessaly and Eperus ; but his authority is hardly sufficiently trustworthy to be received on such a subject. Another proof of the connection of the two ideas is found in the notion, that one of the causes which convert men into vampires after death is the eating the flesh of a lamb that has been killed by a wolf. . . . Without entering further on the question of lycanthropy, we may notice how easy the transition is from the one superstition to the other ; for at a very early period in the history of the Indo-European race the wolf, partly as being the great enemy of shepherds and partly, no doubt, from its sinister appearance and habits, came to be regarded as a representative of the evil powers. Hence the Germans and Slavs have always attributed to the wolf a demon nature ; and M. Wachsmuth tells us that he was informed (though I cannot say that this is confirmed by my own observation)

THE WEREWOLF

that the modern Greeks are in such fear of this animal that they shrink from even pronouncing its name."

I do not know why Mr. Tozer should speak so slightingly of the authority of M. Cyprien Robert, who was the Professor of Slavonic Letters and Litterature at the College de France, a distinguished name and a writer who is held in marked esteem by all other scholars. In his *Les Slaves de Turquie*, vol. i, Introduction,[73] M. Robert writes : " The people of Servia and Herzogivina have preserved more than one dark tradition of unhappy souls who after death are condemned to wander hither and thither over the earth to expiate their sins, or who live a horrid life in death in the tomb as *voukodlaks* or vampires. The *voukodlak* (literally *loup-garou*, werewolf) sleeps in his grave with open staring eyes ; his nails and his hair grow to an excessive length, the warm blood pulses in his veins. When the moon is at her full he issues forth to run his course, to suck the blood of living men by biting deep into their dorsal vein. When a dead man is suspected of leaving his place of sepulture thus, the corpse is solemnly exhumed ; if it be in a state of putrefaction and decay sufficient for the priest to sprinkle it with holy water ; if it be ruddy and fresh-complexioned it is exorcized, and placed in the earth again, where before it is covered a sharp stake is thrust through and through the carcass lest it stir forth once more. Not long since it was customary among the Serbians to riddle the head of the corpse with their bullets and then to burn it entire. This is seldom done now, but they firmly believe that even the carrion crow will shun the living corpse, and wing fast away from such ill-omened flesh. In Thessaly, in Epirus, and among the *Vlachi* of the Pindus district the country-folk believe in another kind of vampire, one which their fathers also well knew in days of old. These *vampires* are living men who in a kind of somnambulistic trance are seized by a thirst for blood and prowl forth at night from their poor shepherd's huts to scour the whole countryside, biting and fiercely tearing with their teeth all whom they meet, man or beast. These *voukodlaks*, who are especially eager to quaff the hot blood of young girls, go to rut—the peasants say—with the *viechtitsa*, a succubus with wings of flame who swoops down in the dark hours upon any fine and gallant fellow as he lies asleep, wellnigh throttling him in their avid caresses and firing him with unbridled lusts. Sometimes, too, the *viechtitsa* in the shape of a hyaena will carry off children into the depths of some fearsome wood."

In his *Macedonian Folklore*[74] Mr. G. F. Abbott writes : " The ' were-wolf ' of English and the ' loup-garou ' of French folklore find in the Macedonian ' wild-boar ' (ἀγριο-γούροννο) a not unworthy cousin. The belief, though not quite so general at present as it used to be, cannot be considered extinct yet. According to it, Turks, who have led a particularly wicked life, when at the point of death, turn into wild boars, and the ring worn by the man on his finger is retained on one of the boar's forefeet. The metamorphosis takes place as follows : the sinner first begins to grunt like a pig (ἀρχινάει νὰ μουγκρίζῃ), he then falls on all fours (τετραποδίζει), and finally rushes out of the house grunting wildly and leaping over hedges, ditches, and rivers until he has reached the open country. At night he visits the houses of his friends, and more especially those of his foes, and knocks at their doors for admittance. He chases with evil intent all those whom he meets in the way, and generally makes himself disagreeable. This he continues doing for forty days, and at the end of that period he betakes himself to the mountains where he abides as a wild beast. . . .

" The Bulgarians hold that Turks who have never eaten pork in life will become wild boars at death. . . . The Bulgarian superstition is practically the same as that of the Melenikiote peasantry, but the latter presents the curious point that the transformation of the Turk into a boar is supposed to occur *before* death and to be gradual. That peculiarity seems to identify it rather with a process of metamorphosis than of metempsychosis, especially as the doctrine of transmigration is so rarely found in Christian countries. . . The Albanians believe in some strange beings which they call *liougat* or *liouvgat*, defined by Hahn [75] as ' Dead Turks, with huge nails, who wrapped up in their winding sheets devour whatever they find and throttle men '.

" Akin both to the above superstition and to [the vampire] is the Wallachian belief in a being called *priccolitsch*."

Mr. J. C. Lawson, in his admirable study *Modern Greek*

THE WEREWOLF

Folklore and Ancient Greek Religion,[76] devotes nearly seventy pages to an account of "the most monstrous of all the creatures of the popular imagination " in the Greek-speaking world, the Callicantzaros (καλλικάντζαρος). The diversities of their outward form are almost endless, but their activities have one feature in common—mischief, although this ranges from dirty practical jokes and boisterous pranks to violent assaults, ravishments, and even blood and murder. The Callicantzaros may be a giant, a mere pigmy, or of the stature of a man, yet all are grotesquely and hideously deformed, in spite of which, as Leone Allacci wrote, "they devour a road at the pace of Pegasus," [77] and they are terrible in strength. Gaunt and lean, with fierce red tongues slobbering from great yawning mouths, set with sharp white fangs, often furnished with thin ropy tails, the bestial form here predominates the human.

The Callicantzari are only active in the night hours and appear but during one set period of the year, the δωδεκαήμερον, the twelve days between Christmas and Epiphany. Leone Allacci, even, assigns them a week, Christmas and the octave.

Local tradition differs as to their exact nature, and Mr. Lawson sums up the matter by saying : "·On the mainland they are most commonly demons ; in the islands of the Aegean, more usually human." [78] Professor Polites, the great Greek scholar, tells us that in Oenoë it is said " they are really evil demons ", whilst in Tenos they declare " The Callicantzari are not demons ; they are men ; as New Year's Day approaches they are stricken with a fit of madness and leave their house and wander to and fro ".[79]

The tradition of Tenos is distinctly supported by Leone Allacci, who says that in the isle of Chios children born in the octave of Christmas are seized with a madness, during which they range up and down the highways. If they meet a wayfarer they ask him " Tow or lead ? " If he answer the former he passes on unhurt ; if he replies " lead " they attack him and leave him half-dead, lacerating him with their nails which grow long and sharp like claws. He adds that children born at this time had the soles of their feet scorched until the nails were singed so they could not become Callicantzari. This cruel custom is exceedingly significant, for a human being who is disposed to scratch will presumably use his hands, whilst a beast will tear with paws and hind-feet as well.

That werewolfism has been mixed up in popular tradition with the ideas of the Callicantzari is very clear, and this becomes even more certain when we find that in Messenia, in Cynouria (east Laconia), and in districts of Crete the Callicantzari are also known as Λυκοκάντζαροι, of which word the first compound is actually λύκος, wolf. Moreover, in parts of Macedonia Callicantzari are often dubbed plain λύκοι, wolves. In Mykonos, too, they have been described as " savage quadrupeds ".[80]

The Callicantzari are not, indeed, werewolves, but in certain districts the idea of werewolfism is a not unimportant factor in the tradition concerning these monstrous beasts.

Even more closely is werewolfism interwoven with the Greek tradition of the vampire. There must, however, in the first place be made a very clear distinction between the vampire and the werewolf. The vampire is a dead body which continues to live in the grave, whence it issues by night for the purpose of sucking the blood of living persons, and thereby indefinitely preserving its vitality and securing the carcass from decomposition. The werewolf is a sorcerer, a living man, who by his pact with hell and demoniacal charms is able to assume the form of a wolf, in which shape he roams abroad giving himself to all the bestial propensities and horrid appetites of that animal.

Nevertheless, as we shall have yet further occasion to remark, the two are not infrequently something confused in tradition and grannam lore.

The history and signification of the word *vrykolakas* have already been dealt with, and it were superfluous to recapitulate these points here. Mr. Lawson writes : " The Slavs brought with them into Greece two superstitions, the one concerning werewolves and the other concerning vampires. The old Hellenic belief in lycanthropy was apparently at that time weak—confined perhaps to a few districts only— for the Greeks borrowed from their invaders their word *vrykolakas* in the place of the old λυκάνθρωπος, by which to express the idea of a ' werewolf '." [81] To this I would only add that even if at one time the old belief in lycanthropy was obscured, such is far from being the case to-day.

THE WEREWOLF

Werewolfism in modern Greece is a very real and hideous thing.

By its very nature this most debased form of sorcery must in modern times be rare, but it would indeed be a mistake to argue that it does not exist, and it is to be found in the remoter districts of Italy as well as in Greece.

Sufficient has, I conceive, already been said with regard to the wolf legends of ancient Rome,[82] more especially as these, deeply interesting as they are, lie something outside our present scope, and need not then detain us here.

At the foot of Mount Soracte in Etruria, in the territory of the Falisci, some six and twenty miles from Rome, there stood of old a sanctuary dedicated to the goddess Feronia, who was probably a deity president over vegetation and the fruits of the earth. Here once a year they held a great fair and festival, to which flocked the whole countryside, aristocrats from the City itself as well as rustics and villagers numberless. In the presence of vast throngs the men of certain families walked barefoot, but without scathe or harm, over the hot glowing embers of a huge fire of pine-wood. These sorcerers, who performed the feat, were known as *Hirpi Sorani*,[83] or Soranian Wolves, and Pliny tells us that in consequence of this function they were exempted by a special decree of the senate from military service, taxation, and any sort of public service or duty. Strabo remarks that they were supposed to be inspired by the goddess Feronia, and the ceremony unquestionably took place at her shrine, in a spot especially dedicated under her name, but according to Vergil and Pliny this ritual was not conducted in her honour, but as an act of worship towards the god of the mountain, whose native name was Soranus, but whom they call by the Greek name Apollo, a detail which is extremely significant as linking up the wolf-men of Soracte with the cult of Apollo Λύκειος—the Wolf.[84] Silius Italicus in the *Punica*, v,[85] speaks of men passing thrice through the fire and carrying in their hands the entrails of the sacrificial victims, a truly wizard touch, since in primitive days these were probably human holocausts. This fire-walking at Soracte was a magic *signum*, or surpassing wonder wrought by the demon's aid. Varro, as cited by Servius, informs us that these fire-walkers anointed the soles of their feet with a certain drug before they trod the furnace, so we have here again an instance of the witches' ointment used in lycanthropic practices.

One of the best-told werewolf tales of all time was related by the freedman Niceros at the splendidly spectacular banquet of his old chum Trimalchio.[86] Thus runs his story : " Some while since, when I was still but a slave we used to live in Small Street, in the house which now belongs to Gavilla. And there, as luck would have it, I fell head over heels in love with the wife of Terentius the inn-keeper ; you all used to know Melissa—she came from Tarentum originally—and a lovely bussing-bit [87] she was too ! Not that I cared for her just for the sake of mutton-mongering and a ride, i'vads ; no, no, I liked her because she was a good honest wench, frank and free. If one ever asked her for anything one never got No for an answer ; if she made a spanker, half of it was mine ; and as far as I was concerned too, every penny that came my way she had the handling of, nor even once did she chouse me of a doit.

" Well, her husband—good man !—died at a little country-house they had, and there I was casting about how to get to her by hook or by crook, for I needn't tell you that you learn who are your real friends when you are in a bit of a fix like that. It so happened that just then my master had gone off to Capua to dispatch some business he was concerned in there, and I of course took advantage of such a fine opportunity. I had no difficulty in prevailing upon a young man who was staying in the house to bear me company for a good bit of the way.[88] He was a soldier, and as lusty a lad as the very deil.[89] Off we set about cock-crow, and the moon was shining as bright as midday. We were on the high road with the grave-stones on either side,[90] when my man turned apart to do his jobs (as I thought) among the monuments, so I sat me down singing away to myself and counting the stars overhead. After a while I looked round to see what my companion was up to, and ecod ! my heart jumped into my very mouth. He had taken off all his clothes and laid them in a heap by the road's edge. I tell you I was as dumped as a dead man, for I saw him piss in a circle all around his clothes, and then hey presto ! he turned into a wolf. Please don't think I'm joking ; I wouldn't tell a lie, no, not for a mint of money. But as I was just saying, in a trice he turned into a wolf, and thereupon he began to howl horribly and rubbed off full tilt into the woods. I didn't know whether I was standing on my head or my heels, and when I went to gather up his clothes, why they had all been changed into stone ! Frightened ! phew ! I was half-dead with fear. None the less I lugged out my porker, and as I made way along I kept thrusting at the haunted shadows, until at last I came to my pretty leman's house. There I tottered in looking like a ghost ; every second I thought I was going to breathe my last ; my eyes were set and staring ; the sweat was pouring down my fork in streams ; it was all I could do to gather my wits. Nobody could be more astonished than Melissa to see me out so late on a night jaunt ; and, ' If you had only been a little earlier,' she said, ' your help would have come in very pudding time. A huge wolf has just broken into the place, and made sad havoc among our sheep and kine. You might think a flesher had been at work with his knife from the blood. Master Wolf didn't get off scot free all the same, for our man gave him a good jab across the neck with a pike.' When I heard all this I couldn't so much as close an eye, but no sooner was it broad daylight than I beat the hoof back to my master's, Gaius, and I hurried (I can tell you) as fast as mine host scours after a bilking cheat. When I got to the place where the younker's rigging had been turned into stone I could see nothing but a horrid pool of blood ! At last I reached home, and there I found my soldier abed, bleeding like an ox in the shambles, whilst the doctor was busy dressing a deep gash in his neck. Then I knew that he was a werewolf,[91] and after that I could neither bite nor sup with him ; no, not if you had killed me for it. Yes ; you can all think what you like of my tale, but Heaven help me never ! if I've told a word of a lie."

There are several points of great interest in this werewolf story, which we may take to be a typical yarn of its day, and which shows how prevalent and rooted the belief in shape-shifting was in Italy during the first century of our era, a belief, moreover, founded on fact. To discuss it at length in all its bearings would require a separate monograph, and I must be content to draw attention to but a few of the most salient details.

In the first place the transformation is effected in the moonlight, which, as we shall see later, in modern Portugal also is considered to play a vital part in such metamorphosis. No magic belt is employed, and no ointment or salve is rubbed over the skin. An essential condition preliminary to the shape-shifting is that the man should strip himself stark naked, whilst his return to the human form appears to be accomplished by his repossession of the clothes he had doffed. That the apparel which he has thrown off should be safeguarded during his appearance as a wolf is a matter of the first importance, and he secures this by a magic rite, by urination in a conjurer's circle around the garments as they lie on the ground.

In very many countries ensorcelling properties are ascribed to urine, and (under certain conditions) to the act of urination. Thus we have a similar phrase in Petronius, *Si circumminxero illum, nesciet qua fugiat* [92] (if I were to piss round him in a circle he would be unable to stir). In Hindostan, as in Italy, urinating in a circle was supposed to be a charm binding one fast, and Richard Pischel quotes an Indian formula of great antiquity (*utûlaparimêhah*), " Das Umharnen des Knechtes." [93] One may compare as a mystic function the Urine Dance of the Mexican Zunis, performed by one of their secret Medicine Orders, the *Nehue-Cue*, a dramatic representation of some half-forgotten wizard rite. [94] The Shamans of Siberia brew and drink a magic potion in which human urine is the chief ingredient. [95] The urine of cows is used for sacred lustrations and worship among certain hill-tribes at the foot of the Himalayas, and holy images are even sprinkled with the magic stream. [96] In Coromandel it is supposed to have supernatural healing properties so that the sick are often laved therewith. [97] Similar beliefs and practices are found among the Huron Indians. [98] Thiers, in his *Traité des Superstitions*, [99] records an old tradition that those who first thing in the morning dip their hand in urine cannot be ensorcelled or harmed by any spell of witches during the day. Thus in some parts of Ireland [100] urine was sprinkled on children suffering from convulsions to rescue them from the clutches of their fairy persecutors. "American boys urinate upon their legs to prevent cramp while swimming."[101] Torquemada says that the ancient Romans had a feast to the mother of the gods, Berecinthia, whose idol the matrons in secret ceremony solemnly sprinkled with their urine.[102]

It may be remarked that in Petronius the werewolf does not turn upon his comrade on the lonely road, but rushes off to a homestead to attack the cattle and sheep. The effects of repercussion are emphasized; the soldier is bleeding copiously from the neck, exactly in the same spot where the farm-hand had wounded the marauding wolf.

No classical author is more frequently quoted by mediaeval— and indeed later—writers on werewolfism than Lucius Apuleius, and by some the *Metamorphoses* or *Asinus Aureus* was even considered to be in every detail an exact record of actual happenings. This, of course, is pressing the point too far, but there can be no question that a very great deal of plain fact is presented by Apuleius in a romantic dress. "Aut indicauit, aut finxit," shrewdly comments S. Augustine [103] with reference to the *Metamorphoses*, implying that there is something more than a substratum of truth under the most extraordinary adventures.

As I have already dealt at considerable length with the *Metamorphoses* twice before in connection with the supernatural, important as this work is, I may be excused if I pass it over rather briefly here.[104]

Born about the year 125, Apuleius was of African origin; *semi-Numida* and *semi-Gætulus* he calls himself. The *Metamorphoses*, his greatest work, was probably written at Rome before he was thirty, soon after he had completed his course of study at Athens. The thread of the main story is, no doubt, borrowed from that Greek tale whence also Lucian took his version Λούκιος, ἤ "Ονος (*Lucius, siue Asinus*), rewriting the original in his own limpid and racy style with all the wit and wickedness of Voltaire. For him the supernatural was no more true and could be no more true than were the pretty adventures of *La Chatte Blanche* or *Babiole* to the graceful Comtesse d'Aubroy. Apuleius, however, was evidently attracted, one might justly say, absorbed by that very quality a sceptic Lucian despised; the occult element with its infinite possibilities would appeal to him as a professed mystic and something more than a dabbler in necromancy and the astral sciences. " In the *Metamorphoses*," it has been admirably said, " a brooding spirit of magic is over the whole narrative."

The main incidents of the transformation will be readily remembered. Lucius, a traveller in Thessaly, the home and cradle of all magic, is the guest at Hypata of an old usurer named Milo, whose wife Pamphile is a notorious witch. The lickerish young gallant intrigues with the wanton Fotis, the serving-maid, who allows him to see her mistress change herself into a bird. In order to accomplish this shape-shifting Pamphile strips naked and carefully anoints herself with a mysterious ointment, smearing her body from head to foot that she may fly off through the air. Burning with curiosity Lucius entreats Fotis to allow him to essay the same experiment. But the wrong unguent is used, and Lucius laments : " After that I had wel rubbed euerie part and member of my bodie, I houered with mine armes, and mooued my selfe, looking still when I should be changed into a bird as Pamphiles was, and behold neither feathers nor appearance of feathers did burgen out, but verely my haire did turne in ruggednesse, and my tender skinne waxed tough and hard, my fingers and toes loosing the number of five, changed into hoofes, and out of mine arse grew a great taile, nowe my face became monstrous, my nosethrils wide, my lips hanging downe, and mine eares rugged with haire : neither could I see any comfort of my transformation, for my member encreased likewise, and without al helpe (vewing euerie part of my poore bodie) I perceiued that I was no bird, but a plaine Ass." [105] This form he can only lose if he eat roses, since this flower alone has virtue to dissolve the magic. During that night the house is burgled, and the thieves loading the ass with their prey drive him to their mountain cave. Adventure follows adventure and episode episode as the picaresque panorama unfolds before our eyes. Some are of the most exquisite beauty ; some are grossly obscene ; some are mere thumb-nail sketches ; some are of consider-able length ; some arise directly out of the main narrative ; some are introduced accidentally ; all are of such sur-passing interest we would not lose a page, no not a line anywhere.

THE WEREWOLF

Finally, owing to a vision of the goddess, during a solemn festival and procession of Isis the ass Lucius is enabled to approach one of the priests, who holds a chaplet of roses, and grasp with his teeth the fragrant garland. Immediately the unsightly and brutal figure leaves him. " For my deforme and Assie face abated, and first the rugged haire of my body fel off, my thick skin waxed soft and tender, the hooves of my feete changed into toes, my hands returned againe, my neck grew short, my head and mouth became round, my long eares were made little, my great and stonie teeth, waxed lesse like the teeth of men, and my taile, which combred me most, appeared no where : then the people began to marvaile, and the religious honoured the goddesse, for so evident a miracle." [106] In humblest gratitude he dedicates his life to the service of the deity, and is initiated among the hierophants of her Egyptian temple. The conclusion, the whole of the eleventh book, rises to a strain of rapturous mysticism, where the words often melt in an ecstasy of Platonic loveliness. " In the *Metamorphoses* of Apuleius the syncretistic cult of the Egyptian goddess expresses itself in terms of tenderness and majesty that would fit the highest worship, and in the concluding prayer of the Apuleian Hermes, an ecstatic adoration of God is manifested in language and thought never equalled, still less surpassed, save in the inspired writers of the Church." [107]

The *Metamorphoses* of Apuleius has a fascination, perverse and baroque as it may often be, which is equalled by few books of any literature. Unbroken is the spell which that decadent mystic has cast upon the ages.

It is quite impossible to believe that any work, which at its close rises to the heights of mystic exaltation and rapture achieved in the eleventh book of the *Metamorphoses*, should be in any part a mere romance. Indeed it is not so ; a profound and mysterious truth throbs through every page, is felt even in the most untoward incidents, in the lightest and most wanton novella.[108]

From the very neighbourhood of Rome itself there is recorded a very striking history of shape-shifting and sorcery, incidents which took place in 1050, during the reign of Pope S. Leo IX. We have this account from William of Malmesbury, who when a boy heard it from an old monk of Acquitaine, a member of the same house,[109] Malmesbury Abbey. Now William, who was born about 1090, was educated and professed in the Benedictine family, and he had certainly completed his *Gesta Regum Anglorum* before 1125. There is no question that the French monk was himself an eye-witness of the strange events which he related to the ardent young English scholar. The history with rubric *De aniculis quae iuuenem asinum uideri fecerunt* is given in liber ii of the *Gesta Regum*, cap. 171.[110]

At the beginning of the reign of Pope S. Leo IX, who ascended the Chair of Peter on 12th February, 1049, there were two old women, hard-drinkers and very lecherous, who kept an inn on the high road to Rome, and if it so chanced that any solitary passenger took his halt there for the night they would change him by their evil craft into a horse, a pig, or some other animal, and so sell him at a price to the next buyer. On a day there came to this house a certain young strolling player, a likely lad, whom they transformed into an ass, and since he was skilled in many tricks they gained much money in this way by exhibiting the wonderful animal, who obeyed their every beck and nod, for so they compelled him by force of their magic. Now the youth had not lost his human reason and intelligence, although he was unable to speak. The rumour spread abroad and many came to see the ass out of curiosity, bringing much traffic to the place. A certain wealthy nobleman who lived not far off was resolved to possess this beast, and he paid a great sum of gold to the old women, who straitly enjoined upon him never to allow the ass to enter the water. Accordingly the animal was consigned to the care of a most watchful and keen-eyed servant, and often at a merrymaking or feast, when the wine flowed red, he would be summoned to the banqueting hall to show his tricks. Howbeit after some time, taking advantage of a momentary negligence, the youth, eluding his keeper, was able to plunge into a lake, and the form of the ass in a moment disappeared as he regained his human shape, revealing what had happened to his whilom keeper, who in his turn reported the matter to his lord. The old women were seized, and upon interrogation confessed their manifold sorceries. The facts were reported to Pope Leo, who could at first scarce believe them to be true. S. Peter Damian, however, investigated the whole case and was soon able to convince the Pontiff.[111]

Many grave and accepted authorities relate this history,[112] and Baptista Fulgosi, in his *Dicta Factaque Memorabilia*, lib. viii, cap. xi,[113] " Recentiora de quibusdam Italicis magis," among the more recent examples mentions this case of enchantment as proven beyond all doubt : " iuuenis ille, qui per magas fœminas, in Asinam conuersus uidebatur, de quo coram Leone pontifice, Petrus Damianus accurate cum disputasset, magicae artis effectum, et non figmentum esse asseruit."

The Blessed Torello of Poppi, a solitary and one of the glories of the Vallumbrosan Order, which habit he took at Avanelleto, was eminent for his power over savage beasts. On one occasion when a wolf had carried off the little son of a poor woman of Poppi, the blessed hermit by his word compelled the wolf to bring the child unharmed to his anchorage where he restored him to the weeping mother. The beast fled into the woods. The Bollandists write : " lupus, quem uulgo Moninum uocant, hoc est humana carne uescentem," " a wolf, commonly called *Moninus*, which is to say a feeder upon human flesh." It may very well be, however, that *Moninus* signifies a Werewolf. Blessed Torello died in 1282, and it is most certain that when the district was plagued by warlocks and werewolves he kept his Poppi free and secure from the onslaughts of these abominations. His feast is upon 16th March, under which day he is noticed by the Bollandists, *Acta Sanctorum*, xvi Martii (tomus ii).

There are few better known examples of lycanthropy than that of the peasant, who dwelt near Pavia, an incident which happened in the year 1541, and which is recorded by Job Fincel.[114]

This unhappy lycanthrope was firmly convinced that he appeared in the shape of a wolf to all who beheld him, and indeed that he was actually a wolf with bestial cravings and appetites. Thus he attacked and killed several persons in the fields, tearing their flesh with his strong teeth. When at last he was captured, although this was not effected without very great difficulty, he maintained stoutly that he was a very wolf, only whereas wolves were hairy outside, his fur grew within his body. Some of the bystanders, showing themselves to be more cruel wolves than he, actually made deep wounds in his arms and legs to test the truth of his frantic imaginings. The poor wretch was consigned to the care of skilled physicians, but he died a few days afterwards.

Writers upon lycanthropy never fail to draw attention to this case, which is indeed sufficiently striking, and became a stock instance, so to speak. Our great English poet John Webster, in that supreme masterpiece, *The Tragedy of the Dutchesse of Malfy*, Act V, 2, 4to, 1623, has thus finely utilized the circumstance. The Marquess of Pescara is inquiring of the Doctor concerning Ferdinand, who is sick :—

> *Pesc.* 'Pray-thee, what's his disease ?
> *Doc.* A very pestilent disease (my Lord)
> They call *Licanthropia*. *Pesc.* What's that ?
> I need a Dictionary to 't. *Doc.* I'll tell you :
> In those that are possess'd with 't there ore-flowes
> Such mellencholy humour, they imagine
> Themselues to be transformed into Woolues,
> Steale forth to Church-yards in the dead of night
> And dig dead bodies vp : as two nights since
> One met the Duke, 'bout midnight in a lane
> Behind St. *Markes* Church, with the leg of a man
> Vpon his shoulder ; and he howl'd fearefully :
> Said he was a Woolffe : onely the difference
> Was, a Woolffes skinne was hairy on the out-side ;
> His on the In-side : bad them take their swords,
> Rip vp his flesh, and trie : straight I was sent for,
> And hauing ministerd to him, found his Grace
> Very well recouered.

Lycanthropy is several times alluded to by the Elizabethan and Jacobean dramatists, and one or two instances, which may stand for many, will perhaps be not altogether impertinent here.

In Ford's *The Lovers Melancholy*, 4to, 1629, Act III, " the Maske of Melancholy " (borrowed from old Burton) is presented before Prince Pallador of Famagosta, and we have (p. 66) : *Florish. Enter Rhetias, his face whited, blacke shag haire, long nailes, a piece of raw meate.*

Rhetias. Bow, Bow, wow, wow ; the Moone's eclipsed, Ile to the Church-yard and sup : Since I turn'd Wolfe, I bark and howle, and digge vp graues, I will neuer haue the Sunne shine againe, tis midnight, deepe darke midnight, get a prey, and fall too, I haue catcht thee now. *Arre.*

THE WEREWOLF

Corax. This kind is called, *Lycanthropia*, Sir,
When men conceiue themselues Wolues.

In the same author's *The Chronicle Historie of Perkin Warbeck*, 4to, 1684, Act V, the last scene, Urswicke, King Henry's chaplain, has the following allusion :—

Thus Witches,
Possest, even their deaths deluded, say
They haue beene wolues, and dogs, and sayld in Eggshells
Over the Sea, and rid on fierie Dragons ;
Past in the ayre more then a thousand miles,
All in a night ; the enemie of mankinde
Is powerfull, but false ; and falshood confident.

A belief in werewolfism prevailed in Italy throughout the seventeenth and eighteenth centuries, and to come down to yet more recent times, Signora Angela Nardo Cibele in her *Zoologia Popolare Veneta*[115] (Palermo, 1887, Curiosità Popolari Tradizionali, Pitre, vol. iv, pp. 92–8, xlii, Lòvo, Lupo) says that to-day in Venice and the district the belief in the *lupo mannaro* is almost vanished, although the older Venetian nursery tales often speak of the hideous werewolf who devours children and flocks. The tradition still lingered, however, in Belluno and the neighbouring hamlets, where I have myself met peasants who firmly believed in and dread the *lupo mannaro*. The local saw has it that a wolf must kill a hundred sheep to slake his thirst in their blood. A Venetian proverb, " La morte del lovo xè la salute dela piégora," implies that the death of a tyrant frees his country.

Curiously enough in the Monferrato district the shadow of an old belief in the werewolf seems to survive in a children's game at Pontelagoscuro, where one player represents the wolf who has to catch one of the other players who stand in file protected by " la direttrice ". The one who is first caught then becomes *lupo*.[116] (Superstitioni Usi et Proverbi Monferrini, Palermo, 1886. *Cur. Pop. Trad.*, vol. iii, pp. 41–2. Giuseppe Ferraro.)

Among the Italians of the Alpine provinces it is believed that the demon can transform himself into a wolf, and the *Fontana del Nobiet* near Cimapiasole is locally regarded as a lycanthropous stream. In Campania old folk say that those who are born on Christmas night, which is seemingly held to savour of irreverence, are compelled to be werewolves throughout their lives during the Octave of the Natale.[117]

49

GREECE, ITALY, SPAIN, & PORTUGAL

Lu Lópe menare (il Lupo mannaro) is greatly feared among the Abruzzi.[118] About Christmastide he may be met with on lonely country roads. He utters the most discordant howls, and in his voice there is something hellish and infinitely horrible as it strikes the ear. It is the custom on Ascension Day, which is kept with especial solemnity, to bless a number of waxen crosses, *capecróce*, and these are regarded as most safe preservatives against witchcraft. They are often affixed to wayside shrines and Calvaries. Should the werewolf as he wanders abroad at night come in sight of one of these his power fails him and he slinks away into the darkness.

In Sicily the belief in the *lupo mannaro*[119] is still quite general. A vast number of ancient superstitions are connected with the animal himself. His howl is known as *rùcculu* or *rùzulu*, and a common proverb says : Master wolf is known by his note, *Lu lupu si conusci a lu rùcculu*. It is still held that a man seen by a wolf is struck dumb, and the phrase *Lu vitti lu lupu* can often be heard. A wolf's skin has extraordinary virtues, and the man who wears one will be full of zest and courage even to audacity. A wolf's foot is a potent charm for colic and other pains. In the Salaparuta district any animal bitten by a wolf is known as *allupatu*, and is henceforward inured to pain. In Nicosia *ulupa* is used of a man who has tasted wolf's flesh, which induces an eternal hunger, *allupamentu* or *lupa*. *Fami di lupu*, a wolf's hunger, is said of a large appetite, and if a man eats heartily he is often asked, *E chi manciasti carni di lupu?* Have you been devouring a wolf? In fable, nursery tale, and local proverb the wolf makes a constant appearance. Thus a crafty sly-boots is said to be *lupu vecchiu*; of two mortal enemies it is remarked, *si sparanu pri lupi. Sà cusu è lu Megghiu! dicia Silivestru a lu lupu*, A rogue and a worse rogue, is an old phrase the exact reference of which is lost in antiquity.

According to the Sicilian tradition a child conceived at the new moon will become a werewolf, as also will the man who on a certain Wednesday or Friday in summer sleeps at night in the open with the moon shining full on his face. In Palermo they say that as the moon waxes to her round the werewolf begins to feel the craving ; his eyes sink deep and are glazed (*si cci'nvitrìanu*), he falls to the earth wallowing in the dust or mud, and is seized with fearful writhings and pangs, after which his limbs quiver and contract horribly,[120] he howls and rushes off on all fours, shunning the light, especially (they say at Menfi) torches, candles, or lanthorns. The lycanthrope dashes to and fro, and will bite anyone whom he may meet in his wild courses. His hideous cries may, however, be heard from afar and all hasten to avoid the wolf-man.

When he first feels the horrid desire he sometimes warns his family or his friends to shut fast the door and windows, and not to open to him however instantly he may call and summon them. There is a belief in Francoforte that if a *lupo mannaro* knocks thrice at his door, the third time it is quite safe to admit him as the access will then be over. It is generally supposed throughout Sicily that by some instinct the werewolf first seeks his own home, and in San Fratello they say that with his long sharp prensile nails he can clamber up a wall or a balcony with horrible agility.

The sight of the wayside shrines fills him with fear and trembling, and before the Crucifix or the Madonna he falls impotent to the ground, which shows that he is in truth possessed of the demon, and that werewolfism is clearly diabolical.

No blow with a stick will injure him, but if he be struck with a knife, especially on the forehead or the scalp, and blood drawn, he will be cured. Some say that if the backs of his front paws or hands are pierced the spell is broken. The blood which flows is black and thick, welling in great clotted gouts, *sangue pazzo*.

In Messina there is a curious tradition that the *lupo mannaro* can be cured if he be struck with a key of a certain shape. In Chiaramonte and Modica, however, they say once a werewolf always a werewolf.

A story is told of an incident which is said to have happened at Palermo, or, as some writers prefer, at Salaparuta. The fact is that two happenings have commingled in one narrative, the setting of which is accordingly placed in different localities. A certain wealthy man, the scion of a noble house, at the full of the moon was seized with lycanthropy, a horrid circumstance only known to one trusted attendant, who was wont during the wild height of his fury to let him rush out abroad, as the fit constrained him, by a secret angiport of the palace into a narrow lane, whence he prowled up and down the piazze of the city, filling all with terror and amaze, for not a man but wondered who this dread werewolf might be, seeing that my lord's face and features were so convulsed and hideously lupine as to be unrecognized even by those of his intimacy and own household. It so chanced that at one plenilune when the werewolf was scouring the midnight streets, there encountered him in his hot chase a young gallant, who perchance flown with wine, or it may be of a natural hardihood, by no means gave the wall but drew his toledo and slashed the foul grinning monster, whose white fangs had already snapped to bite, criss-cross over the slanting forehead. There gushed out great drops of black blood, thick like very pitch, the *lupo mannaro* uttered a long discordant howl of agony, his limbs convulsed, and there broke through the animal the man, whom the juvenal recognized as one of his near and most honoured friends. Since that happy encounter, and owing to the courage of the youth, the whilom lycanthrope was never again attacked by his lupine frenzy, but was thenceforth freed from the evil spell.

In the sestiere del Borgo of Palermo there lived a religious lady of honour and unspotted fame. One night, whilst at her devotions, she heard beneath her window the ominous howling of a wolf. Peeping through the heavy close-drawn curtains she saw in the moonlit court not far below a hideous monster. Gaunt and huge it paced ; from the gaping muzzle set with keen white teeth all arow to rend and tear lolled the great slobbering tongue ; the snout was lifted snuffling the wind with eager appetite. It paused, and then loped forward stealthily, when in a moment by a horrid bound and clambering with demoniac agility it had scaled the loggia itself. Full of courage, and commending herself to Our Lady and S. Rosalie, she took a sharp poniard in her hand and boldly stepped out on to the balcony. With a snarl and a snap the thing leaped up at her, its eyes blazing with hellish fury, its hot fetid breath panting horribly, the foam dripping from its champing jaws. Inspired by Heaven she struck out with all her force, and as the steel cut deep and true into the hairy forehead whence oozed the cruddling black blood, the wolf seemed to shrivel as it fell back and limped swiftly away into the shadows. The next morning there came to her house a majordomo followed by two servants bearing costly gifts of silks and jewelry, rare wines, and a sumptuous regalia. These he prayed the lady to accept on behalf of his master, a Prince of the reigning family, whom by her brave and pious deed she had delivered from his hideous lycanthropy when in his madness he beset her the night before.

To-day one often hears in Sicily of such and such a place that *c'è lu lupunàriu*, the haunt of werewolves, although in a secondary sense the phrase may be used merely to describe any dangerous or unfrequented spot.[121]

Domenico Tempio, a celebrated poet of Catania of the eighteenth century, speaking of a lycanthrope has the following lines in his *La Caristia* [122] :—

> Chistu stranu fenominu,
> Critti lu vulgu ignaru,
> Chi sia un 'atroci bestia
> Chiamata, *Lupinaru*.
> Li picciriddi in sèntirlu
> Fra cupi notti ed atri
> Pri scantu si stringevanu
> In senu a li soi matri,
> E li padri medesimi
> Pri lu spaventu immenzu,
> Lu santu matrimoniu
> Lasciavanu in suspenzu.

As has been previously observed, the Spanish word for werewolf, *lobombre*, is of such rare occurrence that Hertz [123] (although quite erroneously) denied the existence of this term. It is probable that the saving influence of the Church for the most part repressed this bestial and most degraded pravity of the witch. Indeed, although werewolfism is not unknown in Spain, tradition speaks very seldom of this metamorphosis.[124] One of the most remarkable of Goya's pictures,[125] however, shows us four sorcerers, old and hideous, confecting their loathly charms in some mysterious hovel. A fifth warlock, mounted on a besom, is just disappearing by the huge chimney. All four lean atomics are stripped naked, and he who is next to be transvected to the sabbat is already transformed into a wolf, albeit he yet stands erect upon his feet. One of this foul crew stales in a corner. Upon

the earthen floor are two carious skulls and a dish of unguent. From the roof-tree hang noxious herbs and rotting bones.

As might be supposed, werewolfism lingers in the remoter Pyrenees, in the Cantabrian Mountains of the north, and in the Sierra Morena. Mr. Elliott O'Donnell writes : " Though they are extremely rare, both flowers and streams possessing the power of transmitting the property of werewolfery are to be found in the Cantabrian mountains and the Pyrenees." [126]

A very ancient and widespread tradition concerns itself in Portugal [127] with the *lobis-homem*, who are for the most part believed to be ensorcelled by some stroke of fate, *fado*, or slaved by a spell, *sina*. The Portuguese *lobis-homem* of the southern province differs in many respects from the were-wolf, for he is a clandestine and even a timid creature. The man (or woman) who is under the charm of the wolf goes out by night to some lonely spot, generally where four cross-roads meet. After having turned round five times with giddy speed, he falls upon the earth grovelling and howling. (If by chance some wild animal has previously lain upon the spot he will assume the shape of that animal.) He then rises transformed to a wolf. But unlike the northern werewolf and the loup-garou the *lobis-homems* seek to harm none. They run about country lanes, but at the least glimmer of a light they gallop off at full tilt into the kindly darkness. If they prowl near a cottage they utter long howls and a kind of sobbing noise, which is taken to be an entreaty for the candle or lamp to be promptly dowsed. M. Ferdinand Denis [128] says that werewolfism seems to have been most prevalent in Portugal in the fifteenth century, but if a belated peasant chanced to meet one of these hapless wretches he had only to strike a flint or show the glim of the lanthorn he was carrying and the *lobis-homem* fled.

A curious point is that the *lobis-homem* was generally supposed to have a short tail, which was covered with yellow fur.

There was, however, quite another and most evil kind of *lobis-homem*, who seems to have been closely connected with the *bruxa*, the Portuguese witch, a Satanist of the vilest and most deadly courses.

Writing in 1870, Oswald Frederick Crawfurd [129] says that

in Portugal "the superstitions have the peculiar gloomy stamp of the legendary mysteries of ancient Italy. . . . The type of Latin legend to which I refer, is that well-known and most grisly and hideous of all ghost stories, the tale of the soldier in Petronius Arbiter. Now the belief in the ' Lupus-homem ' is very prevalent in parts of Northern Portugal . . . [and] nowhere is this belief invested with so many peculiar and gloomy circumstances as in Portugal".

He relates a werewolf history which was told him by a farmer at whose manor he received the generous hospitality of the country. When a young man this farmer was working at a farm, near Cabrasam, among the mountains of Estrica, one of the wildest districts of Portugal. The master of the farm had recently married a young wife, and as the time drew near for their first child to be born it became necessary to engage a woman to help in the many household duties. Accordingly the young hand was dispatched to the nearest town, Ponte de Lima, with orders to hire the first strong young serving-wench he should meet. As he jogged along the road it so chanced he saw sitting by the wayside a likely girl wrapped in a brown cloak with whom he entered into conversation. She gave her name as Joana, and said that she was from Tarouca in the mountains of Beira. Her object was to look for a good situation as a servant in the district. It seemed exactly to jump with the young fellow's mission, and accordingly he suggested that she should present herself to his master. This she did, and although the farm-folk thought that there was a strange look about her, inasmuch as she seemed sturdy and willing she was engaged, and took the mistress' place for a while, undertaking the cooking and housework.

In due time the child was born, a fine healthy boy, made much of and lavishly admired by all the neighbours with the single exception of one old lady, a wise woman, who looked askew when she saw the babe, but on being pressed, in a few moments said plainly that the child was under a spell. All laughed, but the old lady maintained the Devil's mark could be found on the babe, and sure enough between the shoulder blades there was a tiny crescent or half-moon, which looked as though it had somehow been tatooed there and appeared indelible. Now the mirth changed to consternation, but the wise woman cheered the wondering parents kindly enough, only she straitly counselled them to watch the cradle carefully during the time of the new moon, since (said she) there was no cause for anxiety at any other season. This accordingly was done, and as two or three months went by nothing happened.

It was casually remarked that from the first the serving-wench, Joana, exhibited the greatest animosity toward the old lady, and whenever she visited the house the new maid was sure to be abroad or else sat in a dark corner nursing the sullens with her big brown cloak pulled right over her face. Nothing was said since the lass was known to be extremely hot-tempered, and when in a fury her eyes, which were curiously narrow and slanting, would literally blaze fire as she snarled out angry words. To her master and mistress she was always respectful, and not unnaturally before long she became the complete confidante of the latter.

One morning the mistress even entrusted her with the secret the wise woman had disclosed, to her vast surprise, and the girl replied : " Alas, indeed, it is only too true, I have known it a long while, only I feared to tell you. Children with that mark grow into *lupis-homems* unless it is prevented before they reach sixteen."

" Can anything be done then ? " eagerly inquired the mistress. " Why, yes, there is a way. You must cover the mark with the blood of a white pigeon, strip the child naked, and lay him on a soft blanket on the mountain-side the very first time the new moon rises in the heavens after midnight. Then the moon will draw the mark up through the blood, just as she draws the waves of the sea, and the spell will be broken."

In order to save their boy from the fearful doom of the *lobis-homem* the farmer and his wife, after some talk, decided to follow this advice. There happened to be a new moon some few days later, and accordingly, accompanied by the servants whom they apprised of their plan, they laid the babe sleeping in his blanket in the warm summer night on the slope of a hill near the house, whilst the thin silver sickle of the moon yet tarried below the horizon. This done, they returned indoors, for no eye must see the working of the magic charm.

The farmer, it is true, had expressed himself uneasy lest

there should be wolves near, but his men reassured him, since for many a long year no trace of a wolf had been seen in the whole neighbourhood for many miles around. Nevertheless, he got down his old blunderbuss and rammed it with rusty nails for lack of other ammunition. Hardly had he loaded when piteous cries were heard from the spot where the child was lying. All rushed out of the house to see in the light of the new moon just riding above the mountain crest a huge brown wolf, gaunt and lean, standing over the body of the babe. The animal's hot fangs dripped with blood, and the narrow eyes were lit with the fires of hell.

The distracted father fired as the beast was silently slinking away, and it fell, rolling over with a long-drawn howl, just before it could gain the shelter of the wood. The farmer's lad, who wielded a stout club, ran forward to finish it, but only succeeded in dealing the beast a heavy blow on the foreleg as it shuffled yowling and limping into the darkness beyond.

The child was dead, its throat hideously mangled, and the blanket soaked with blood.

When the tiny body had been borne sadly back to the house it was remarked that Joana was not with the company, and indeed had not been seen for some little time. Then the horrible truth flashed upon all—the girl was an accursed witch, a whore of Satan, and as a wolf had killed the child for some black purpose of her own. At earliest dawn the men followed the track of the wounded wolf into the wood, and not ten paces from the place where the animal had dragged itself away was Joana lying on the ground covered with blood. She immediately declared that she had hidden behind the trees to watch the child, fearing some harm, that she heard its piteous cries and ran out as the moon rose, only to see the wolf bounding forward from the covert. At the sound of the gun it had turned and fled unscathed in the confusion, whilst she received the full discharge, and fell wounded. These, of course, were lies suggested by the Devil. She could not explain how her right arm was bruised and wellnigh broken where the lad had struck the blow with his stick, moreover did he not (as he himself swore) see Joana's own eyes glaring in the wolf as the animal wheeled in fury ?

GREECE, ITALY, SPAIN, & PORTUGAL

In charity they sent for the priest, but she died ere he could reach the spot, and they buried her where she lay. Before the earth was thrown on her body the wise woman who came to see it pointed out that the girl had the mark of the *lobis-homem* on her breast quite plainly, and was evidently one of Satan's wolf-pack, a witch of long continuance. She added that if she could have seen the girl's eyes she would have known at once what the evil wench was, for all *lobis-homems* acquire the long narrow eyes and savage look of the wolf. She further explained that if a *lobis-homem* can kill a newly-born child and drink the warm blood, the charm is broken and they are *lobis-homems* no more.

The priest, who had not till then been apprised whence the new servant came, declared that the farm-folk were fools and worse to have anything to do with a woman from Tarouca, for it was just a foul nest of warlocks and witches.

FOOTNOTES:

¹ 105. Teubner, Lipsiae, 1894, ed. Dietsch and Kallenberg, p. 368.
² *De Chorographia*, recognovit Carolus Frick, Teubner, 1880, p. 31. I quote the translation by Arthur Golding, *The Rare and Singuler worke of Pomponius Mela*, London, *Anno* 1590, p. 39. Solinus, also, merely echoes the older authorities, and has nothing to add. He writes, xv, 7 : " The Neuri indeed, as we are told, at certain seasons are transformed into wolves, and then after a given time, assigned by lot, they recover their original form. *C. Iulii Solini Collectanea Rerum Mirabilium*, Iterum Recensuit Th. Mommsen, Berolini, 1895, p. 82.
³ *Die Indogermanen, Ihre Verbreitung, Ihre Urheimat, und Ihre Kultur*, 2 vols., Strassburg, 1905 ; vol. i, p. 120.
⁴ *Reise um die Erde durch Nord-Asien und die beiden Oceane in den Jahren 1828, 1829 und 1830*, Berlin, 1833, i, p. 232 : " Es scheint nämlich kaum zu bezweifeln, dass die bei Herodot, nicht nach eigner Ansicht sondern nach indirekter Überlieferung, ausbewahrte Erzählung : ' die Neuren werden alljährlich während einiger Zeit in Wölfe verwandelt ' (Herod. iv, 105) ganz einsach auf winterliche Bekleidung mit Thierfellen sich beziche."
⁵ Pausanias's *Description of Greece*, tr. by Sir J. G. Frazer, six vols., London, 1898 ; vol. i, Introduction, p. xvii.
⁶ Eusebius, *Praepartio Euangelica*, x, 9 : " Πρῶτος δὲ Κέκροψ λέγεται Ζῆνα κεκληκέναι τὸν Θεόν, μὴ πρότερον οὕτω παρ' ἀνθρώποις ὠνομασμένον." Migne, *Patres Graeci*, xxi, 809.
⁷ VIII, i, 4 ; ii, 1, 2, 3. Frazer, vol. i, pp. 373–5.
⁸ For the cult (both in East and West) of S. Elias the Prophet, the Father of the Carmelites, see the Bollandists, *Acta Sanctorum*, under 20th July, the Feast of the Prophet. *Iulii Tomus V*, folio, Antwerp, 1727, *De S. Elia Propheta*, i, ii, and iii, pp. 4–10. G. F. Abbott, *Macedonian Folklore*, 1903,

THE WEREWOLF

pp. 240-1, remarks that the highest summits of mountains are generally dedicated to S. Elias and are often chosen for his shrines. Mr. J. C. Lawson, *Modern Greek Folklore*, 1910, p. 44, speaks of " S. Elias whose chapels crown countless hilltops ", and adds in a note, " I am unable to determine whether this Saint is the prophet Elijah of the Old Testament, or a Christian hermit of the fourth century. The Greeks themselves differ in their accounts." An error has crept into popular belief in some places. It is the Prophet S. Elias (not the holy hermit), to whom the shrines on the hills are dedicated.

⁹ By many primitive folk the shadow is conceived of as being the soul, or at least a vital part, of a man. For various modern Greek superstitions connected with the shadow see Bernhard Schmidt, *Das Volksleben der Neugriechen*, Leipzig, 1871, pp. 196 sqq., also more generally Frazer, *The Golden Bough*, vol. iii (*Taboo*, 1927), pp. 77-96.

¹⁰ Frazer's *Pausanias*, op. cit., vol. i, pp. 423-4.

¹¹ *The Early Age of Greece*, vol. ii (1931), p. 474.

¹² V. Bérard, *De l'origine des cultes Arcadiens*, pp. 49 sqq. Philippe Berger, *Revue des Deux Mondes*, 1896, cxxxviii, p. 386. See also Immerwahr, *Die arkadischen Kulte*, p. 14 sqq.

¹³ Thus Statius, *Thebaïdos*, iv, 275 :

Arcades huic ueteres astris lunaque priores.

Cf. Pliny, *Nat. Hist.*, vii, 48 and 49 ; also Ovid, *Fasti*, i, 469-70 ; ii, 289-90, " Arcades, et luna gens prior illa fuit " ; also the Scholiast on Apollonius Rhodius, iv, 264 ; upon Aristophanes, *Nubes*, 398.

¹⁴ Thus Ausonius, *Technopægnion*, De Deis, l. 8, has : " Mænalide Pan." Ovid, *Fasti*, iv, 649-50 : " Silua uetus . . . Stabat, Mænalio sacra relicta Deo." On which Burmann glosses : " *Maenalius Deus*, Faunus, quem passim poetae Latini cum Pane, Deo Arcadum, confundunt."

¹⁵ III, viii, 1. *Bibliotheca*, ed. E. Clavier, Paris, 2 vols., 1805 ; vol. i, pp. 317-321.

¹⁶ Dionysius of Halicarnassus, i, 13, says Lycaon had twenty-two sons ; Pausanias, viii, 3, counts the tale as twenty-seven.

¹⁷ He gives the name of Maenalus twice over. Delete the repetition and supply Melaneus, also add Oenotnes.

¹⁸ Ed. Mauricius Schmidt, Jenae, 1872, p. 30. Fabula clxxvi.

¹⁹ l. ii, c. iv.

²⁰ 8.

²¹ Ed. Kinkel, Teubner, 1880, p. 21. For the notes see pp. 113 and 114.

²² Nonnus in his *Dionysiaca*, xviii, 20 sqq., and Arnobius, *Contra Gentes*, iv, 24, both say that Nyktimos was sacrificed. So also Clement of Alexandria, *Protrepticon (Cohortatio ad Gentes)*, cap. ii : Λυκαων ὁ Ἀρκὰς, ὁ ἑστιάτωρ αὐτοῦ, τὸν παῖδα κατασφάξας τὸν αὐτοῦ (Νύκτιμος ὄνομα αὐτοῦ) παραθείη ὄψον τῷ Διί. Migne, *Patres Graeci*, t. viii, 113-16.

²³ Orelli, *Hist. Excerpt.*, Leipzig, 1804, pp. 41 sqq.

²⁴ ll. 211-239. I quote Dryden's translation. "*Examen Poeticum* : Being The Third Part of Miscellany Poems," London, 1693, pp. 18-21, from " The First Book of Ovid's Metamorphoses, Translated into English Verse by Mr. *Dryden* ".

²⁵ *The History of the World*, two tomes, folio, London, 1601, " Translated into English by Philemon Holland," tome i, p. 207. For the original text of this particular passage I have used *C. Plinii Secundi Naturalis Historiae, Libri XXXVII*, ed. Carolus Mayhoff, Teubner, 1904 ; vol. ii, pp. 105-6.

²⁶ The edition of Pliny " Apud Hackios, A° 1669 ", vol. i, p. 516, has " Fabius " in the text without comment.

²⁷ i, 29.

²⁸ *Solon*, xi.

²⁹ i, 1063-5.

³⁰ Quintilian, *Instit. Orat.*, x, 95. See also S. Augustine, *De Ciuitate Dei*, vi, 2, where the Saint quotes Cicero in praise of Varro's learning, also a line from Terentianus Maurus :

Uir doctissimus undecumque Uarro.

GREECE, ITALY, SPAIN, & PORTUGAL

In the *De Ciu. Dei*, iii, 4, Varro is spoken of as " uir doctissimus eorum (i.e. paganorum) ".

[31] *Etymologia*, VIII, ix, 5.

[32] *C. Iulii Solini Collectanea Rerum Memorabilium*, vii, 21. Iterum recensuit Th. Mommsen. Berolini, 1895, p. 57.

[33] " Sacrifice " in *Encyclopædia Britannica*, ninth edition, vol. xxi, 1886.

[34] *The Cults of the Greek States*, Oxford, vol. i (1896), p. 41.

[35] *The Early Age of Greece*, vol. ii (1931), p. 475.

[36] *Über den Zeus Lykaios*, Progr. des Gymnasiums zu Göttingen, 1851, pp. 38 sqq.

[37] *Dictionnaire des Antiquités* ; Daremberg, Saglio, and Pottier. Paris, 1904. Tom. iii, deuxième partie, fascicule 31, pp. 1432–7.

[38] Deuteronomy, xii, 2. For the consecration of mountain tops to Zeus (Ύπατος) see Dr. Farnell, op. cit., 1896, pp. 50–1, and the notes p. 152 with illustrative quotations. The lewd cult of these Baals is described by J.-A. Dulaure, *Des Divinités Génératrices*, Paris, 1805, ch. iv (new ed., Paris, 1905, pp. 55–62) ; Julius Rosenbaum, *Geschichte der Lustseuche im Alterhume*, English translation, Paris, 1901, vol. i, pp. 49–64.

[39] *Geographica*, ed. Aug. Meineke, Teubner, 1895, vol. ii, pp. 549–50. C. J. Groskurd in the introduction to his edition of Strabo, 3 vols., 8vo, Berlin and Stettin, 1831–3, judges that Strabo died about A.D. 24. It should be remarked that the temple of Zeus Lykaios had neither statue nor treasury.

[40] Pausanias, VIII, xxxviii, 3.

[41] Eng. tr., ut sup., p. 147.

[42] Eng. tr., ut sup., pp. 74 and 75.

[43] Eng. tr., ut sup., pp. 19–22.

[44] See the *Malleus Maleficarum*, part ii, qn. i, ch. 13 : *How Witch Midwives commit most Horrid Crimes when they either Kill Children or Offer them to Devils in most Accursed Wise*. Eng. tr., pp. 140–4. Also Guazzo, *Compendium*, II, xv ; Eng. tr., pp. 135–6.

[45] For Leukas see Strabo, 452 (ed. ut cit.) ; Aelian, *Nat. An.*, xi, 8 ; Photius, *Lexicon*, ed. S. A. Naber, Leyden, 1864–5, s.u. Λευκάτης. For Kourion in Cypus, Strabo, 683. See also Ovid, *Ibis*, 467–470, for a probable allusion to human sacrifices to Apollo at Abdera, " Urbs Thraciae initio anni hominem deuouet pro salute communi, obruitque lapidibus " ; *Ouidii Opera*, Oxonii, 1826, vol. v, p. 504.

[46] For the cult of Apollo Λύκειος, see Farnell, *Cults of the Greek States*, Oxford, 1907, vol. iv, chapter iv, pp. 112–124 and notes ; Ridgeway, *The Early Age of Greece*, vol. ii, pp. 475–7 ; Frazer, *Golden Bough*, Spirits of the Corn and of the Wild, vol. ii (ed. 1925), pp. 283–4, " Wolf Apollo " erroneously, or at least partially, explained as Apollo the " Wolf-slayer " ; also Frazer, *Pausanias*, vol. ii, pp. 195 sqq., for wolves in connection with Apollo ; Andrew Lang, *Myth, Ritual, and Religion*, 1887, vol. ii, pp. 199–201.

[47] Op. cit., vol. iv, p. 114.

[48] For Leto as a she-wolf see Aristotle, *Hist. An.*, vi, 35 ; Scholiast on Apollonius Rhodius, ii, 124, ἤματι χειμερίῳ πολιοὶ λύκου ὁρμηθεντες, who tells us that the wolf was honoured at Athens ; Aelian, *Nat. Anim.*, iv, 4, and x, 26 ; Antigonus, *Historiarium Mirabilium collectanea*, 56 (61) in *Scriptores rerum mirabilium Graeci* (p. 77). ed. A. Westermann, Brunswick, 1843. Servius on Vergil, *Æneid*, iv, 377, speaks of Apollo as a wolf.

[49] Aristotle, p. 580a, 17 : " ἐν τοσαύταις ἡμέραις τὴν Λητὼ παρεκόμισαν οἱ λύκοι ἐξ Ὑπερβορέων εἰς Δῆλον, λύκαιναν φαινομένην διὰ τὸν τῆς Ἥρας φόβον."

[50] Diodorus Siculus, v, 56 (from Xeno Rhodius) ; Antoninus Liberalis, *Transformationum congeries*, 35, in Westermann, *Scriptores* (ut sup.).

[51] iv, 101 and 119. The epithet is incorrectly explained by Autenrieth, *Homeric Dictionary* (English ed. by R. P. Keep, 1896), p. 198 : " λυκη-γενέϊ, (lux), *light-born*, epithet of Apollo as sun-god." Liddell and Scott are doubtful, for they say " commonly explained *Lycian-born*, i.e. at Patara ", ed. 1897, p. 906. Many of the older scholars were doubtless misled by Macrobius, *Saturnalia*, I, xvii, who derived Λυκηγενής from λύκη, dawn. He writes :

61

THE WEREWOLF

" Antipater Stoicus Lycium Apollinem nuncupatum scribit . . . Cleanthes Lycium Apollinem appellatum notat, quia ueluti lupi pecora rapiunt ita ipse quoque humorem eripit radiis," a striking example of far-fetched and much-mistaken ingenuity.

[52] *Iliad*, iv, 119.

[53] According to Servius on Vergil, *Æneid*, iv, 377 : " (Lycius Apollo) siue quod est λευκός a candore, idem enim et sol creditur, siue quod transfiguratus in lupum cum Cyrene concubuit : siue quod in lupi habiter Telchinas occiderit . . ." The Telchines are represented under different aspects, but the most general accounts speak of them as sorcerers of Rhodes or actual demons who had the power to assume any shape they pleased, and could bring on hail, storm, and snow. Ovid, *Metamorphoseon*, vii, 365–7, follows a tradition which says they were destroyed by Jupiter in a deluge on account of their malignancy, for they possessed the evil eye :—

Telchinas,
Quorum oculos ipso uitiantes omnia uisu
Jupiter exosus, fraternis subdidit undis.

Uitiare, i.e. *fascinare*. They were βάσκανοι.

[54] See Pindar, *Pythian*, ix, 5 ; Apollonius Rhodius, ii, 500–7 ; Diodorus Siculus, iv, 81. Apollo at Keos was himself called Aristaios (*Ἀρισταῖος*). See also Pindar, *Pyth.*, ix, 63 ; and Servius on Vergil, *Georgics*, i, 14.

[55] The Scholiast on Sophocles, *Electra*, 6.

[56] Farnell, op cit., vol. iv, p. 115.

[57] Aelian, lib. xiii, cap. 40 : " Τιμῶσι δὲ ἄρα Δελφοὶ μὲν λύκον." Clement of Alexandria, *Cohortatio ad Gentes*, 30 : Λυκοπολῖται δὲ λύκον [σέβουσι]. Migne, *P.G.*, vol. viii, 120.

[58] ii, 124.

[59] *Bulletin de Correspondance hellénique*, 1895, p. 12, an inscription of the fifth century B.C. Pausanias, x, 14, 7. Eusebius, iii, 14, 5 (from Porphyry, περὶ τῆς ἐκ λογίων φιλοσοφίας) :

ἀνὰ δ' ἐξέθορες, μάντι Λυκωρεῦ,
τόξοτα Φοῖβε.

Also see Plutarch, *De Pythiae oraculis*, xii.

[60] Apollodorus, 1, 9, 15 ; Euripides, *Alcestis*, the opening of the play, Apollo's speech ; Tibullus, II, iii, 11–28 ; *Georgics*, iii, 2. Cf. Aeschylus, *Septem*, 145 :

Λύκει' ἄναξ, λύκειος γενοῦ στρατῷ δαΐῳ.

Cf. also *Iliad*, xxi, 438, and the Homeric Hymn to Hermes, 22, 70, etc.

[61] The Scholiast on Demosthenes, xxiv, 114.

[62] Pausanias, ii, 9, 6.

[63] 10, 1. τοὺς λύκους ὁ 'Απόλλων προοίμιον λοιμοῦ ποιεῖται . . . εὐχώμεθα οὖν 'Απόλλωνι Λυκίῳ τε καὶ Φυξίῳ.

[64] *Lex Salica*, 58 : "*wargus* sit—hoc est, *expulsus* . . ." Cf. the Old Norman Laws, Laws of Canute, Laws of Henry I, as quoted later in Chapter IV.

[65] " Circum quaque etiam in cultu daemonum luci succreuerant, in quibus ad huc eodem tempore infidelium insana multitudo sacrificiis sacrilegis insudabat." *Uita S. Benedicti*, auctore S. Gregorio Magno, cap. 11. Bollandists, *Acta SS.*, die xxi Martii. Tom. iii (Martii), Antverpiae, folio, 1668, p. 280 F.

[66] No. 196 : ed. Karl von Halm. Teubner, 1889, pp. 97–8.

[67] Fincel does not appear in Moréri's *Grand Dictionnaire Historique*, nor yet in the *Nouvelle Biographie Générale*. There is, however, a brief notice, which I have supplemented, in N. F. J. Eloy's *Dictionnaire Historique de la Médicine*, 4 tomes, Mons, 1778 ; vol. ii, p. 233. The *Wunderzeichen* is not even recorded by Graese or Caillet.

[68] Francofurti, 1612. Pars iii, pp. 153–7. Fincel's elegiaes are skilfully turned and not without poetic and personal feeling.

[69] 2 vols., 1869, vol. ii, ch. xxi, pp. 82–4.

[70] Curt Wachsmuth, *Das alte Griechenland im neuen*, Bonn, 1864, p. 117 : " Hier tritt also, wie es scheint, deutlich hervor die sonst bei den neugriechischen Wrukolaken nicht mehr erkennbare Natur des Werwolfes . . . S. Weleker kleine Schriften, iii, S. 187 ff. (*Lykanthropie ein Aberglaube*

und eine Krankheit) ; Otto Jahn, über Lykoros in den Berichten der sächs. Ges. der Wiss. ; 1847, S. 423 ff. ; vgl. im Allgemeiner Hannsel, die Werwölfe in der Zeitschr. f. deutsche Mythol., iv, S. 193 ff.

[71] Arthur und Albert Schott, Walachische Märchen, Stuttgart and Tübingen, 1845, p. 298.

[72] Les Slaves de Turquie, Serbes, Monténégrins, Bosniaques, Albanais et Bulgares. Édition de 1844, Paris, 2 vols. 1852, vol. i, p. 69.

[73] Ibid., pp. 68–70.

[74] Cambridge, 1903, pp. 215–17.

[75] J. G. von Hahn, Albanesische Studien, Jena, 1854 ; i, p. 16.

[76] Cambridge, 1910. For the Callicantzari see pp. 190–255.

[77] De Graecorum hodie quorundam opinationibus Cologne, 1645, cap. ix.

[78] Op. cit., p. 209.

[79] Παραδόσεις, i, p. 344, being part ii of the series Μελέται περὶ τοῦ βίόυ καὶ τῆς γλώσσης τοῦ Ἑλληνικοῦ λαοῦ.

[80] Lawson, op. cit., pp. 216–19.

[81] Ibid., p. 384.

[82] See for further details the chapter " Der Wolf " (pp. 158–177) in Otto Keller's Thiere des Classischen Alterthums in Culturgeschichtlicher Beziehung, Innsbruck, 1887.

[83] Festus, De Uerborum Significatione, lib. ix, Amstedolami, 1700, p. 193, has : " Irpini appellati nomine lupi, quem irpum dicunt Samnites."

[84] Pliny, Nat. Hist., vii, 19 ; Vergil, Æneid, xi, 784 sqq., with the glosses of Servius who quotes from Varro ; Strabo, v, 2, 9 ; Dionysius Halicarnasensis, Antiquit. Roman., iii, 32. See also Frazer, The Golden Bough, Balder the Beautiful, vol. ii, ed. 1923, pp. 14 sqq., and The Dying God (1923), p. 186. Festus tells us that the Samnites were guided by a wolf. L. Preller, Römische Mythologie, 3rd ed., Berlin, 1881–3 ; i, 268, follows G. Curtius (Grundzüge der griechischen Etymologie, 5th ed., Leipzig, 1879) in linking up the first syllable of Soranus and Soracte with the Latin Sol (sun), which is impossible.

[85] ll. 175–181. Andrew Lang mentions the Hirpi in his Myth Ritual and Religion (1887), vol. ii, p. 213. See further, W. Mannhardt, Antike Wald- und Feldkulte, Berlin, 1877, pp. 327 sqq. He compares the rites of the Soranian wolves with the ceremonies of the Norman fraternity of the Green Wolf at Jumièges. (In no part of France was werewolfism more prevalent of old than in Normandy.) Frazer (Balder the Beautiful, chapter vi, 2, " The Meaning of the Fire-Walk ") regards the fire-walk as a charm to dispel the incantations of malevolent witches and as a preservative from spectres. This may be true in some instances, but the Hirpi Sorani were themselves witches and wolves.

[86] Petronii Satirae, tertium ed. Franciscus Buecheler, Berolini, 1895 ; 61, 62, pp. 40–1.

[87] pulcherrimum bacciballum.

[88] ut mecum ad quintum miliarium ueniat.

[89] fortis tanquam Orcus.

[90] The Roman custom being to bury by the side of the roads. " The tombs were ranged on either side of the roads leading from the towns . . . The forms of the monuments are very varied." J. E. Sandys, A Companion to Latin Studies, Cambridge, 1910, p. 183.

[91] intellexi eum uersipellem esse. Baring Gould, The Book of Were-Wolves (1865), pp. 64–5, says that uersipellis " resembles the Norse hamrammr ", the idea being that the skin is reversed or turned inside out, for which he quotes the case of the countryman at Pavia as related by Job Fincel. This, however, is certainly incorrect, for the notion that the werewolf when in human form is merely wearing his wolf's pelt with the fur turned inside, and to change his shape he has but to uncase and reverse, is not contained in uersipellis.

[92] 57 ; ed. cit., p. 37.

[93] Zu Petronius, Satirae 62. No. vi in Philologische Abhandlungen. Martin Hertz zum siebzigsten Geburtstage von ehemaligen Schülern dargebracht. Berlin, 1888, pp. 69–80.

THE WEREWOLF

[94] Described by Captain J. G. Bourke in his *Compilation of Notes and Memoranda bearing upon the Use of Human Ordure and Human Urine in Rites of a Religious or Semi-Religious Character*, Washington, 1888, pp. 8–10.

[95] Schultze, *Fetichism*, New York, 1885, p. 52.

[96] J. Shortt, " Notes on the Hill Tribes of the Neilgherries," *Transactions of the Ethnological Society*, London, 1868, p. 268. See also Moor, *Hindu Pantheon*, London, 1810, p. 148.

[97] Bernard Picart, *Coûtumes et Cérémonies Réligieuses de Tous les Peuple der Monde*, Amsterdam, 1729, vol. vii, p. 28.

[98] Père Gabriel Sagard, *Histoire du Canada* (new edition), Paris, 1885, p. 107.

[99] Paris, 1741, tom. i, c. 5, p. 171.

[100] John Brand, *Popular Antiquities*, London, 1849, vol. ii, p. 86, " Christening Customs," also James Mooney (Bureau of American Ethnology), *Medical Mythology of Ireland*, Washington, 1887.

[101] J. G. Bourke, op. cit., p. 47.

[102] " La rociaba con sus orinos," J. de Torquemada, *Monarquia Indiana*, Madrid, 1723, lib. x, c. xxiii. See also lib. vi, cs. xiii and xvi.

[103] *De Ciuitate Dei*, xviii, 18.

[104] *The Geography of Witchcraft*, 1927, chapter i, pp. 27–31 ; *The Vampire in Europe*, 1929, chapter i, pp. 42–52. I have not hesitated to quote pretty freely from my two former books here.

[105] *The eleuen Bookes of the Golden Asse . . . Translated out of Latin into English by William Adlington*. London, 1596, chap. 17, p. 53.

[106] Ibid., chap. 47, p. 197.

[107] Father Cyril Martindale, S.J., article " Paganism ", *Catholic Encyclopædia*, ed. New York, 1913, vol. xi, p. 393.

[108] Traube, Munich Academy, *Abhandlungen, Philosophisch-Philologische*, Classe, xix, 308, writes on the popularity of Apuleius in the middle ages.

[109] " quodam loci nostro monacho genere Aquitanico aetate prouecto arte medico in pueritia audisse me memini." Lib. ii, cap. 170 (ed. Stubbs, p. 198).

[110] *Gesta Regum Anglorum*, ed. W. W. Stubbs, Rolls Series, vol. i (1887), pp. 201–2.

[111] S. Peter Damian amongst other instances referred to the instances of Simon Magus and Faustinianus. S. Peter Damian, Doctor of the Church, Cardinal-Bishop of Ostia, 1007–1072.

[112] Amongst others, Matthew Paris, O.S.B., *Chronica Maiora*, ed. Luard (Rolls Series, 1872–1883), i, 518–19 ; *Flores Historiarum*, ed. H. R. Luard (Rolls Series, 1890), i, pp. 567–8 ; Roger of Wendover, O.S.B., *Flores Historiarum*, ed. H. O. Coxe (English Historical Society, five vols., 1841), i, pp. 485–6 ; John Brompton in Roger Twysden's *Historiae Anglicanae Scriptores X*, folio, 1652, column 940 ; Radulfus Niger, *Chronicon*, ed. Robert Anstruther, Caxton Soc., 1851, pp. 155–6 ; Vincent of Beauvais, *Speculum Naturale*, lib. ii, cap. cix, Venice, folio, 1591, tom. i, p. 26 ; Ulrich Molitor, *De lamiis et pythonicis mulieribus*, 1489, cap. iii ; Bodin, *Démonomanie*, ii, 6, 1580, p. 100 (verso), misprinted 80 ; Boguet, *Discours des Sorciers*, 1590, xlvii (Eng. tr. *Examen of Witches*, 1929, p. 142) ; Petrus Thyraeus, S.J., *De Spirituum Apparitionibus*, cap. xv, 222, ed. 1594, p. 114 ; *A Pleasant Treatise of Witches*, 1673, pp. 22–3.

[113] Ed. 1509 : sig. ll ii (pages not numbered).

[114] Thence by Simon Goulart, *Thrésor d'histoires admirables et memorables de nostre temps*, 2 vols., 12mo, Paris, 1600, and quoted by many other authors. By some untoward confusion of ideas John Webster, whose singularly futile *Displaying of Supposed Witchcraft*, London, 1677, quotes Fincel to disprove the possibility of werewolfism, p. 33. Webster has other allusions, pp. 68–9, p. 86, and pp. 91–106, which are not worth citing. Webster, of course, does not entirely deny the supernatural ; he is sufficiently sane to be cautious. Ed. 4 vols., 8vo, Genève, 1620, vol. ii, Lycanthropie, pp. 720–1. Simon Goulart of Senlis, a Lutheran minister and prolific compiler, was born 20th October, 1543, and died 3rd February, 1628. Goulart's work in question was translated into English by Edward Grimeston, *Admirable and Memorable*